Jenny Oldfield

DOLPHIN ISLAND

Missing

Illustrations by
Daniel Howarth

Hodder
Children's
Books

For lovely Lola, Jude and Evan – three dedicated dolphin fans

HODDER CHILDREN'S BOOKS

First published in Great Britain in 2018 by Hodder and Stoughton

1 3 5 7 9 10 8 6 4 2

Text copyright © Jenny Oldfield, 2018

Inside illustrations copyright © Daniel Howarth, 2018

The moral rights of the author and illustrator have been asserted.

A CIP catalogue record for this book is available from the British Library.

ISBN 978 1 444 92831 0

Typeset in ITC Caslon 224

Printed and bound in Great Britain by Clays Ltd, Elcograf S.p.A.

The paper and board used in this book are made from wood
from responsible sources.

Hodder Children's Books
An imprint of Hachette Children's Group
Part of Hodder and Stoughton
Carmelite House
50 Victoria Embankment
London EC4Y 0DZ

An Hachette UK Company
www.hachette.co.uk

www.hachettechildrens.co.uk

Chapter One

Mia Fisher sat by the campfire in Base Camp Bay smiling from ear to ear.

"'Happy birthday to you!'" Her brother, Alfie, and sister, Fleur, yelled out the words. "'Happy birthday, dear Mi-mi, happy birthday to you!'"

The sun was sinking in a vivid orange sky – Mia's favourite colour. It made the waves dance and sparkle and lit up the happy face of the birthday girl.

'Happy birthday, honey-bunch.' Mia's dad, James, gave her a big bear hug then swung her round until she was dizzy.

'Whoa!' she gasped. Her hazel eyes were alive with happiness and wisps of brown hair, lightened by the sun after more than forty days on Dolphin Island, stuck to her hot cheeks.

Her mum, Katie took her by the shoulders and steadied her. 'Seven years old today. Who'd have dreamed you'd be spending your birthday surrounded by palm trees and white sands?' A wistful look passed across her suntanned face as she squeezed Mia's hand. 'We all thought we'd be back in old England in the rain and cold.'

'Stuck in a classroom behind a boring old desk,' Alfie said with an exaggerated frown.

'Stacking the dishwasher and tidying our rooms,' thirteen-year-old Fleur added. 'Instead, here we are!' She pointed to the cliff behind them rising to Lookout Point and the tree-covered mountain beyond. Then she swept her arm towards the azure sea with its dancing waves breaking against the reef at the edge of the bay.

'We're in the middle of the South Pacific, miles from anywhere.' Alfie threw fresh wood on to the fire and watched the sparks fly upwards. 'Doing what we like when we like – beachcombing and building stuff ...'

Mia's head had stopped spinning so she skipped down the beach a little way then turned to face him. '... Like shelters?'

'Yes, building shelters and keeping the fires going, making a dugout canoe ...'

'... Swimming with dolphins!' Mia interrupted again as she ran on towards the sea.

'Where?' Fleur sprinted after her, scanning the ocean for the first signs of Jazz, Stormy and Pearl, their fantastic dolphin friends. Alfie threw another branch on to the fire then followed them.

Mia stopped at the water's edge. 'Nowhere. I'm just saying what my favourite thing about the island is – swimming with Stormy and playing games with him.'

'Oh.' Fleur turned down the corners of her mouth. 'I thought you'd spotted them swimming this way.' She saw a white heron rise from the dark reef and flap towards Turtle Beach headland where small storm petrels waded in shallow rock pools searching for crabs. But there were no telltale fins rising to the surface, no shiny domed heads and sleek grey bodies entering the bay. Fleur quickly got over her disappointment. 'Anyway, Mi-mi, you left the party early. Alfie hasn't had time to give you your present yet.'

'Ooh, what is it?' Mia clapped her hands.

'It's … hey, watch out!' Alfie warned as she turned her back on the incoming tide. A large wave hit her from behind, sweeping her off her feet.

Fleur and Alfie rushed to drag the birthday girl on to dry land. Fleur rescued Mia's straw hat floating in the water then jammed it on her head.

'I'm going back to base camp for Alfie's present,' Mia reminded them. She marched, sopping wet, towards where the fire burned brightly in the shadow of the overhanging cliff.

Halfway up the beach, Alfie caught up with her and delved into the pocket of his red shorts. 'Here – I brought it with me. I haven't had much time to make this for you. I hope it's OK.' Shyly he handed her a small object carefully wrapped in a shiny green leaf.

Mia shook water from the brim of her hat then took the gift. 'Do you know what it is, Fleur?' she asked as she turned it over and started to unwrap it.

'Yes, I saw him making it.' Fleur knew Mia would be thrilled. Alfie was clever with his hands and he'd used his special knife to carve the present, sitting cross-legged on Echo Cave Beach, where he was sure Mia wouldn't find him.

Mia's fingers fumbled with the piece of blue string that Alfie had used to keep the wrapping in place. Then she took out a softly shining, flat object and held it up to the firelight. 'It's a tiny dolphin!' she murmured. Alfie had carved it out of a piece of mother-of-pearl. It was about four centimetres long and hanging from another length of thin blue string.

'I made you a lucky charm,' Alfie explained nervously. He couldn't tell from Mia's face whether or not she liked it. In fact, from where he stood, it looked as if she was about to cry.

Tears welled up in Mia's eyes as she turned the carved dolphin this way and that. It glowed a creamy colour, with glints of pink and pale blue. Her bottom lip trembled.

'Don't be upset,' he pleaded with a worried look. 'If you don't like it, I can make you something else.'

She clasped the dolphin in the palm of her hand. 'No – I love it,' she whispered. 'These are happy tears.'

'See – she loves it,' Fleur echoed. She felt that Alfie's gift put her own birthday present to shame. It was a fan made from bird of paradise and cockatoo feathers, hastily put together earlier that day, in between fetching water from Butterfly Falls and throwing logs on to the lookout fire. 'Alfie's present is for good luck, Mi-mi. You have to keep it with you wherever you go.'

'For ever and ever,' Mia promised as she wiped away her tears. 'Please will you tie it around my neck?' she asked Fleur.

'Now who wants a birthday pudding made out of mashed-up jackfruit and sugarcane?' Katie called.

'Me! Me! Me!' Three voices shouted as one.

'And who wants to play pass the parcel?' James asked.

'We all do!' Fleur yelled. She looked forward to a fun evening – munching gooey treats, playing party games, singing and dancing as the sun sank below the watery horizon like a burning disc of gold. Even though their last shelter had burned down in the Big Fire that had rampaged across the island only four days earlier and they'd had to start building everything all over again, the Fishers were determined to give the youngest member of their family the best birthday party ever.

*

The sun had gone down and the moon and stars shone in a clear sky. Fleur's stomach was full as she strolled down to the shore, leaving Mia already fast asleep in George's Cave. By the light of the moon eleven-year-old Alfie used a stone hammer and his knife to chip away at the canoe they'd started to hollow out from a tree trunk – one of the few things at base camp that had escaped the disastrous wildfire. Their dad was busy collecting stones at the foot of the cliff, planning to build a food store to keep their fish and fruit safe from marauding monkeys, while their mum had already begun her night shift at Lookout Point, keeping the fire there alive.

The sound of the ocean filled Fleur's head – the everlasting roar of breaking waves and the suck of pebbles as they ebbed. A cool breeze blew her long brown hair back from her face as she stood ankle-deep, trying to block out memories of birthdays back home – real Victoria sponge cake with jam and cream, big bowls of cheese and onion crisps, and hot dogs snugly wrapped in soft bread rolls. *With lashings of tomato ketchup,* she thought with a sigh. *So much for trying not to think about home.*

In her mind's eye she pictured the Fishers' pretty riverside house, with Gran and Granddad living next door. Home had things that she'd once taken for granted: a roof that didn't leak, proper glass windows and brick walls. A real bed with a soft mattress and a cosy duvet. A toilet that flushed, hot running water, shampoo ...

'Are you OK?' Alfie had come up behind her and now spoke in a low murmur.

'Yep,' she nodded without turning her head.

'What're you thinking about?'

'Nothing.' *Scented shampoo that disappears down the plughole in a white, soapy stream, leaving your hair silky soft. Giant fluffy towels, Mia in her panda onesie, snuggling under the duvet, pleading for a bedtime story.*

'You're wishing we were at home.' Alfie bent to pick up a pebble then skimmed it across the silvery water. Four bounces then *plop* – it vanished without trace.

'How did you guess?'

'Easy-peasy.' Forty-one days stranded on a tiny island in the middle of the Pacific made everyone homesick, especially on a special occasion like a birthday. 'I always know what you're daydreaming about when you wander off by yourself.'

Fleur sighed. 'Do you think Mia had a good time today?'

'Yep.' Alfie skimmed another pebble. Six bounces then *plop*.

'She loved your lucky charm.'

'And your fan.'

'I'll make one for you if you like.' Fleur looked sideways at him and grinned.

'No thanks.' Brightly coloured feathers weren't Alfie's thing – or Fleur's. They preferred plain old palm leaf fans any day.

Together they stood for a while and gazed out to sea. Then Fleur broke the silence. 'Alfie, do you think we'll ever leave Dolphin Island?'

He didn't answer straight away. 'Yeah – once we've finished the canoe,' he said hesitantly.

'What then?' Fleur knew that it would only be big

enough for two people. 'Who'll go off in it and try to find help?'

'Mum and you maybe?'

'Or you and Dad?' Another picture came to mind of Alfie and their dad paddling off in the tiny canoe, out on to the big ocean, heading south towards Misty Island. Waves and wind, thunder and lightning, danger all around; Fleur's unruly thoughts made her shiver.

Alfie shrugged. 'Anyway, the canoe is nowhere near finished so we're stuck here for a bit longer. And there's still lots to do.'

He and Fleur turned away from the water. They walked up the beach towards the cave where Mia lay on her new sleeping platform with Monkey, her bedraggled soft toy. Fleur's pet gecko, George, kept watch from his ledge, occasionally flicking out his long tongue to catch spiders. Beyond the cave they crossed another stretch of white sand then skirted wide of the campfire to approach the bushes and palm trees growing at the base of the cliff.

'Lots to do.' Fleur echoed Alfie's words as she came close to the burnt-out shell of their old shelter. The fire started by the macaque monkeys had left hardly anything untouched. Flames had destroyed the thatched roof and the walls made from panels of woven palm fronds. Practically every single thing they owned, apart from a few metal objects like knives and pans, had collapsed into a heap of grey ashes. Gone was their map of the island painstakingly drawn on to a scrap of sailcloth, their notched calendar stick, the clothes that they'd salvaged from sunken *Merlin* – all gone.

'But our new shelter will be bigger and better,' Alfie promised. He clenched his fist, flexed his muscles and showed her his biceps. 'Look – Superman!'

He made Fleur laugh. 'At least we know how to build one now.' They'd learned that it was best to hammer strong stakes into the ground and build a raised bamboo platform for the shelter to stand on. And now they knew which palm fronds to choose for the best weaving material. They'd learned how to lash the panels securely to upright poles so that the wind didn't blow the walls down. A watertight roof was the most important thing of all. So she, Mia and Alfie had already trawled Turtle Beach and Echo Cave Beach for suitable materials – plastic sacks, pieces of old sails – anything waterproof they could find among mounds of rubbish washed on to the shore.

Fleur stepped up on to the half-built platform, her face glowing in the firelight. 'I reckon we should head south to Pirate Cave Beach first thing tomorrow,' she suggested quietly. 'See if we can find anything useful there.'

'Yeah, like more plastic containers for collecting water. We have to replace the old ones.' Alfie knew that the route would take them past a small grove of bamboos, which always came in handy in any case.

'Early,' Fleur insisted, her mind still on the building work. 'Before it gets too hot.' Bigger and better – a shelter built of driftwood and bamboo canes, palm fronds and grasses, with stone steps leading up to the front door, an awning to provide shade and a separate, stone-built food store that the monkeys couldn't raid.

'Deal,' Alfie agreed. He fed the campfire then yawned. 'I bet I'll be awake before you.'

'No you won't.' Fleur jumped down from the

platform on to the sand then strode off towards their temporary sleeping quarters in George's Cave. 'You'll still be snoring when I'm up and dressed.'

He overtook her at a slow jog. 'How much do you bet?'

'One conch shell and two cockatoo feathers.'

'Deal,' he said again, bumping knuckles with Fleur as he tiptoed into the cave.

Chapter Two

'You owe me one conch shell and two feathers.' Alfie won the bet. He woke before sunrise and jabbed Fleur in the ribs with his elbow.

'Yeah, yeah,' she groaned, her eyes still closed. 'What time is it?'

He looked at his bare arm in the grey dawn light. 'By my watch it's five hairs past my wrist.'

'Uh-uh-uh,' she sighed. 'Very funny.'

'Come on, wake up – it's getting light. Time for our recce,' he hissed. Mia was still asleep and their dad had already left the cave to switch places with Katie high on the ledge above the cliff. It was their mum's turn to catch a few hours' sleep and she would soon be crossing the beach to join Mia.

So Fleur rolled over and crawled out of the cave.

'Bye, George,' she whispered when she spotted him on his ledge.

The little green gecko twitched his tail and watched them leave.

'I don't know what you see in him,' Alfie began as they made their way towards the shadowy headland where the white heron still kept watch. It stood on one leg, gazing out to sea. 'Geckos aren't much fun. They just sit there and stare.'

'No they don't,' she argued. 'Actually, they're very interesting. For a start, they can't blink so they have to lick their eyes to keep them clean. They can see in the dark. And they make a chirping noise when they talk to each other.'

'Sorry I spoke.' He pulled a face as he reached the rocks and began to climb them. Knowing his wildlife-crazy sister, she would go on about geckos non-stop all the way to Pirate Cave Beach.

'I love the suction pads on their toes,' she enthused. 'It means they can walk across ceilings. And they shed their skin every four weeks or so – like snakes.'

'Yuck – now I really wish I hadn't mentioned it.' The

heron rose up from the rock then flapped away. Down on the new beach, three turtles made their weary, waddling way into the water, where they soon floated off. 'Look over there – monkeys!' He pointed to a stand of bamboos growing at the edge of the beach.

Sure enough, a little band of macaques emerged from the greenery. They were hard to see in the half-light but their quick movements caught Alfie and Fleur's attention and they paused to watch them pick up coconuts then bash them against a nearby rock to break their shells. A young one got separated from his mother until she screeched at him and he ran back to her.

'You're only making me look at the monkeys to stop me talking about geckos.' Fleur grinned then marched on.

'OK then, what about dolphins?' Alfie changed the subject again. The rising sun cast long shadows across the white sand. Slowly the sky turned from misty pink to bright blue.

'What about dolphins?' Fleur looked eagerly out to sea, only to be disappointed once more. There was nothing there except the heron flapping lazily towards the reef.

'Which do you like better – geckos or dolphins?'

'Both,' she said without stopping to think.

'No – which?'

Loyalty to cute little George tugged at Fleur's heartstrings but then she thought of Jazz, her loving, lovely dolphin who adored cuddles and who talked to her with his high-low whistle and took her on high-speed rides far out to sea. 'OK, you win,' she admitted. 'It's no contest. Of all the species on this planet, dolphins are far and away the best.'

*

Mia was waiting on the shoreline for Fleur and Alfie to come back. The sun was high in the sky and the sand was too hot to walk on so she stood in the shallow water and felt the waves lap around her ankles.

She'd already built a sandcastle and dug a deep moat to watch the incoming tide fill it up. Then she'd practised skimming stones the way Alfie had taught her – hold the stone flat between thumb and forefinger then with a flick of the wrist fling it far out to sea. Her best effort was five bounces – her highest score ever. Now what should she do? She could go for a swim to cool down, but there was a Dolphin Island rule not to go swimming alone in case you got caught by a strong current and swept out to sea. And that was never mind the danger of the tiger shark coming back. This was the worst thing that could happen, Mia knew. A tiger shark could grab you with its sharp teeth and bite your arm off. No – she'd better stay where she was and carry on waiting.

She stood on one leg the way herons did. Then she flapped her arms and pretended to fly. She wished she had super powers like Wonder Woman. She switched legs, watched and waited.

Oh! Out past the reef she saw a movement. She stared hard – one fin, then two and then three cut through the blue water. *Three dolphins!* Was she imagining it? The waves swelled and rolled towards the shore. The fins drew nearer. One of them was more curved than the others – that must be Alfie's Pearl leading the way. Yes – the young dolphin's head broke the surface – grey on top and pinky-pearl underneath.

Her mouth curved upwards in a smile, as if she was pleased to see Mia waiting for her on the shore.

'Hiya, Pearl!' She rushed waist-deep into the water and waved both hands above her head.

Alfie's dolphin slapped her tail against the water and made a big splash.

'Hiya, Jazz, hiya, Stormy!' Mia cried as they circled around her.

Jazz rolled on to his back, inviting her to tickle his pale grey tummy. A jealous Stormy nudged Mia with his beak. He gave a single, shrill whistle to tell her that he too wanted a stroke.

Laughing, she flung her arms around him. 'Don't worry, I still love you the best,' she told him as she plonked a kiss on his round head.

He blew water out of his blowhole and it showered down on her, making her squeal and giggle. Then he nudged her again, to show how pleased he was to see her.

'Guess what – I'm seven!' she told him as she clambered on to his broad back and held on to his dorsal fin. 'It was my birthday yesterday. Alfie gave me this present.' Leaning forward to show him her lucky charm, she lost her balance and fell into the water.

The three dolphins circled, churning up the shallow water by slapping their tails. They gave chirps of delight then little clicks and whistles, inviting Mia to come and play.

'I'm waiting for the others,' she tried to explain as she hauled herself on to Stormy's back once more. 'Here they are!' She pointed towards the headland where Fleur and Alfie had appeared, loaded down with an old car tyre and three plastic containers. Alfie had a coil of rope slung from his shoulder and Fleur wore a white plastic sack as a cape.

'Alfie, Fleur – here I am!' Mia yelled at the top of her voice. The dolphins too whistled their greeting. 'Look who's come to play!'

Alfie stood on the headland and stared down into Base Camp Bay. 'Do you see what I see?' he asked Fleur with a sudden burst of joy.

She didn't stop to answer him. 'Jazz!' she yelled at the top of her voice, dumping her plastic bag and water containers on the rocks before sprinting to the furthest point then diving straight into the deep, cool water. When she surfaced, she came face to face with her very own dolphin.

Jazz, with his downturned mouth and dark shading around his eyes, nudged her shoulder and invited her to come aboard.

Alfie was hard on Fleur's heels. He too flung himself headlong into the water then swam out from the rocks, only coming up for air when he saw Pearl's pink belly directly above him. He surged upwards through a cloud of bubbles and broke the surface, gasped air into his lungs then clambered on to her back. 'Hi, Pearl!' Holding her fin with one hand, he leaned forward to rub her velvety head with his knuckles.

She slapped the water with her tail flukes then played a trick on him by rolling on to her back and turning full circle.

'Hey!' Alfie held on tight and got a mouthful of salty water. He bobbed back up to the surface still gripping Pearl's dorsal fin.

Mia thought that it looked like fun. 'Do that to me,' she pleaded with Stormy.

He ignored her and set off at top speed towards the reef. Unable to resist a race, Jazz and Pearl soon followed. They almost drew neck and neck with the speedy leader, carrying their riders with ease.

'Stormy and me are the winners!' Mia exclaimed at the crescent of jagged rocks where their boat *Merlin* had come to grief. 'This is the finish line – we won!'

The race through the water had brought Fleur back to life after the hot, sticky walk from Pirate Cave Beach. Salty water dried quickly on her skin and made it tingle. A cool breeze felt good against her face as she sat astride Jazz and patted his smooth sides. 'We let her win, didn't we?'

Next to her, Pearl repeated her rolling trick, dunking Alfie in the cold, clear water for a second time.

He gulped as he came up, still holding tight. 'OK, Pearl, enough rolling for today. I've found something new for us to play with.' He let go of her fin then slid from her back, taking a small neon-green plastic object from his pocket. He trod water and let her approach. She eyed it carefully then nudged his hand with her beak.

'It's a referee's whistle,' he told her. 'It was washed up on the beach.'

'Hey, let me see!' Mia plunged sideways from Stormy's back into the water then swam towards Alfie.

'Get ready to listen to this – it makes a funny noise,' Fleur whispered to Jazz.

Alfie put the plastic whistle to his lips and blew. The shrill, piercing sound rose above the low, steady roar of the waves. An excited Pearl raised her tail flukes and slapped the water. Stormy put back his head to let out a series of sharp, quick clicks while Jazz carried Fleur in a wide circle until they came back to where they'd started.

'Here – you have a go.' Alfie handed the whistle to Mia.

She gave three sharp blasts. Stormy answered with a single, long whistle of his own. Then he rose out of the water and did a spectacular tail-walk around them while Pearl blew out through her blowhole with a loud, rasping raspberry noise that made Alfie laugh. Jazz came in close and nudged Mia's arm.

'Do you want to know what's making that funny sound?' Fleur murmured as she slid into the sea. 'It's

23

something new, isn't it? We can play a game with it if you like.'

The three dolphins grouped together and watched.

Fleur explained the game she'd invented. 'Mi-mi, you blow the whistle. Alfie – we hold our noses then duck down underwater when we hear it. We count to five then we come up. We'll do that a few times – OK?'

'What for?' Mia wanted to know. She bobbed up and down in the waves, with the reef behind her and beyond that the wide horizon under a clear blue sky.

'To see if the dolphins can learn to copy us.'

So Mia blew the whistle and Fleur and Alfie disappeared below the surface. The curious trio watched. Fleur and Alfie came up on the count of five.

'Again!' Alfie gasped.

They did it a second time and then a third. At the fourth blow of the whistle, when Fleur and Alfie plunged downwards, the dolphins flicked their tails and joined them underwater.

'Three – four – five!' Fleur faced Jazz under the water, her hair fanning out behind her, eyes staring straight into Jazz's face. Then up they rose, back to the

surface, reappearing at exactly the same time as Alfie, Stormy and Pearl.

'Yay!' Mia cried. She raised her hands and clapped. 'They did it!'

'How cool was that?' Fleur grinned at Alfie.

'Very cool.'

The dolphins swirled around them, clicking excitedly.

'Whistle!' Mia held it high out of the water and pointed to it as if they would understand the word. She thought that this was the best game ever and wanted it to go on.

But now something called the dolphins away. They regrouped by the edge of the reef, heads close together, looking out to sea.

Mia, Fleur and Alfie followed the direction of their gaze. Far out from the shore, a pod of dolphins breached the water and soared through the air; more than a dozen of them – fully grown adults and young calves playing in the sparkling waves. Some made a clean arc and landed with scarcely a splash while others flipped over and threw themselves backwards into the water, creating white spray as they landed. They swam parallel to the horizon, on their way to a new feeding ground and calling for young Pearl, Jazz and Stormy to join them.

'Go!' Fleur called. 'Don't get left behind.'

So their three friends chirped their farewells then set off at breakneck speed towards their pod without swerving or fooling around, intent on obeying orders from their elders. They cut cleanly through the water without a backwards glance.

Mia handed the whistle to Alfie then sighed and turned for the shore. She swam doggy-paddle, every now and then glancing over her shoulder to see if Stormy had changed his mind.

'I guess it's their lunchtime.' Alfie swam alongside her while Fleur struck out ahead. 'They're probably hungry.'

'Me too,' Mia realized as she switched to front crawl. Fleur was already wading out of the water and making her way back to the headland to collect her morning's beachcombing haul. 'Bagsy I play with that car tyre first,' she called as Fleur hoisted it on to her shoulder to carry it back to camp.

Chapter Three

'I realise we shouldn't be pleased that piles of rubbish get washed up on to our beaches.' Alfie was hard at work on the new shelter, using some of the rope he'd found that morning to lash together lengths of bamboo that would finish the platform on which it would stand. 'It's not nice to look at but at least we find lots of useful stuff amongst it.'

Fleur agreed and glanced up at the conical, tree-covered mountain that loomed over the whole island. 'This rope means we don't have to go into the forest to look for more lianas.' Jungle creepers were useful for tying things together, but, after what she'd seen and heard up there before the Big Fire had destroyed half of the island, she wanted to put off venturing in there for as long as possible.

'Not for a while at least.' Alfie tied the last knot then stood back to judge his work. 'Are you still having bad dreams?'

'A few,' she admitted. It made her hands shake to remember the sight of a family of wild boars squealing as they fled from the dark shade of the forest into blinding sunlight then raced down the slope towards Lookout Point. Their flight had been followed by a rumbling, hissing sound that emerged from the shadows. Then came the snapping branches, the heavy footfall ... But whatever it was hadn't come out of the forest. 'How about you?'

Alfie's nightmares were about shipwrecks. In his dreams he relived the moment during the storm when their boat had crashed into the reef – the crunch of *Merlin*'s hull against rock, the sudden tilt of the deck as he tried to cling to the guardrail but lost his grip, the battering force of the waves, wind and rain. 'Not so many,' he told Fleur, distracted by the sight of Mia rolling the big car tyre down the beach. She looked funny and cute at the same time in her turquoise swimmie and a grass skirt that Katie had made for her as a birthday present. There were yellow and red feathers sticking out of her hatband and she wore strings of shells as a necklace over her new lucky charm.

'So will you come with me when we have to go back?' Fleur sat in the shade weaving a sleeping mat out of palm fronds. This one would be for their dad, to save him from getting bitten by pesky sand hoppers in George's Cave.

'Into the forest?' Alfie checked.

'Yes. I don't want to go by myself.' She held her hand poised over her work and tried to stop it shaking. Nothing else on Dolphin Island scared her – not the fat, hairy millipedes that could be twenty centimetres long or the cane toads croaking out their chorus by Butterfly Falls. Not even the big tusks of the wild boars had bothered her, once she'd got used to the idea that they shared their island with them. No – it was the unseen, hissing monster that had been hunting the boars that she dreaded.

Alfie frowned as he searched the base of the cliff for big, flat stones that would make steps up to the platform. 'Maybe the fire killed it – whatever it was.'

'Yes, maybe.' Fleur hadn't considered this. 'Not if it stayed in the forest though. The flames didn't reach that far.'

'But the smoke did.' He tried his best to make Fleur feel better. 'My guess is that, whatever this monster thing is, it made its way over to the other side of the island where it was safe.'

She took a deep breath and carried on weaving. 'Let's hope so,' she said. 'And let's hope it stays there and doesn't come back.'

'Here – help me carry this stone.' He'd found one that was exactly the right size and shape.

Fleur took one end and together they lifted it and staggered a few steps until they could place it in position by the newly built platform. By the time they'd done this, Mia had abandoned the tyre at the shoreline then cartwheeled her way back up the beach.

'Hey,' Alfie protested when he saw what she'd done. 'Don't leave it there – the waves will drag it back into the sea and we'll lose it.'

'Wait here. I'll get it.' Fleur sprinted down to the water's edge to retrieve the tyre. From a distance the new platform looked good but it would be many days before the shelter was finished – perhaps by Day 50 if they worked flat out. She glanced up to Lookout Point, where James was stacking wood for the fire, then across at the headland between Base Camp Bay and Echo Cave Beach to see Katie patiently fishing for crabs in the rock pools. That would be supper – crab meat roasted over the fire, followed by sun-dried jackfruit and slices of coconut.

Fleur ducked to avoid a flock of noisy red and green parrots that swooped low across the bay, then she picked up the tyre and carried it up the beach. *I know what to do with this*, she decided. *We've got some spare rope so I'll find a tree with a low branch and make a swing for Mia to play on*. The thought pleased her so she picked up speed. 'I've had a great idea,' she called as she drew near.

*

The sun set that night in its usual fiery glow and rose next morning a misty pink. In the gentle dawn light Mia used Alfie's knife to make a new notch in the calendar stick jammed into the sand outside George's

Cave. She did the same on the next day and the one after; awake before anyone else to mark the start of the forty-fifth day on Dolphin Island.

Putting a notch in the calendar stick was Mia's special job. They'd begun a new one straight after the fire and Alfie also had hopes of drawing a fresh map of the island on a piece of sailcloth that he'd stashed away on Turtle Beach. They would use charcoal to mark the bays on the east coast, right down to Mangrove Bay and Land's End in the south, with Misty Island lying offshore amongst a string of islets strung out like green jewels in an azure sea. Map-making and marking the days were important – second only to building a shelter and keeping their two fires alight.

So Mia made the notch carefully on the upright stick and was about to go and play on the new swing before breakfast when she paused and looked up at the sky. She thought she'd heard a sound over the breaking waves – it was different from a parrot's squawk or a pigeon's coo, coming from very high up, in amongst the mist that clung to the mountain top and drifted down the slope towards Lookout Point. It was a continuous, light rumbling noise, but not thunder because there were no dark clouds. Puzzled, she went on staring and didn't notice Alfie crawl bleary-eyed out of the cave then stand up with a yawn and a stretch. Then he too heard the far-off noise and snapped his mind into focus with a sudden start and a loud grunt.

'Plane!' he muttered, screwing up his eyes and staring at the mountain. 'Guys, there's a plane! Dad, Fleur – wake up!'

They jerked awake and shot out of the cave to join Alfie and Mia. James wore a sweatshirt and denim shorts. Fleur was in her dad's T-shirt, that came down to her knees. Her hair was loose around her shoulders.

'Plane,' Alfie repeated. 'Listen!'

Though they couldn't see it, the sound was unmistakable. It was getting louder, coming their way.

'Quick – we have to build up the fire!' Fleur was the first to move. She raced up the beach, kicking up the cool white sand, then tore at the stack of firewood to throw new branches on the embers. It had to roar with orange flames and send up clouds of smoke before the plane reached them.

With his heart hammering against his ribs, Alfie sprinted after her. 'We've got to make the pilot see us!'

Down by the cave, James had a different idea. 'You stay with me, Mia.' He yanked the calendar stick out of the ground. 'We'll use this to write "Help!" in giant letters in the wet sand. Your mum will be able to signal from Lookout Point. Between us we'll let him know that we need to be rescued.'

A plane – an actual plane, the first they'd seen for many days. Alfie and Fleur built up the base camp fire, while high on the ledge, Katie did the same.

'Surely, this time!' Fleur whispered, crossing her fingers tight as at last the plane emerged from the mist.

Alfie recognized it straight away – a small private jet with a T-tail and twin engines mounted far back on the fuselage. 'Looks like a Cessna. There's room for one pilot and four passengers.'

Shielding her face from the heat of the flames, Fleur stepped back from the fire and stared up at the plane. 'Five people. One of them has to see us!'

'Make the letters huge.' Down at the water's edge, Mia pleaded with her dad. 'Write them bigger so they can see.'

He wrote the 'H' with the end of the stick, digging deep into the wet sand to make it clear and easy to read. Then 'E', then 'L' and 'P'.

The plane crawled slowly across the sky, leaving a thin trail of white vapour behind it as the pilot held a steady course from west to east.

'Look this way – down here!' Mia jumped up and down on the spot while James craned his neck and muttered a prayer.

The little Cessna plane could mean rescue. Every member of the Fisher family clung to the white vapour trail as if it were a thread that would pull them back into their old, familiar world of family and friends. They would no longer wake each morning to begin the hard struggle to survive on the fish they managed to catch and the fruit they found here on this beautiful uninhabited island. They would be able to call a doctor when they were sick and wake up every day in a clean, warm bed. They would wear shoes again and go to school on the bus.

'Please!' Fleur held her breath. The two fires blazed and black smoke spiralled upwards. She closed her eyes, not daring to look.

The Cessna flew in a straight line, high over the lookout ledge, over the cliff face and the burnt-out shelter, over the beach where Mia stood with her dad.

'Look down!' Alfie's knuckles were white as he clenched his fists.

On it went, its engines roaring steadily. They saw its belly with the undercarriage tucked out of sight, the smooth underside of its wide, white wings.

'Help!' Mia cried.

Out by the reef, three dolphins appeared. They swam quietly at the surface without approaching the shore.

Charting a straight course above the scattered islands, the pilot travelled on. Perhaps she was studying her instruments instead of noticing her surroundings, or perhaps she was a he and he was on autopilot and too busy chatting with the passengers in the seats behind him. Onwards they flew, towards the rising sun.

On the beach below, excitement drained away and left everyone feeling empty and hopeless. Mia cried as a wave came in and washed away their plea for help written in the sand. Alfie unclenched his fists. Fleur sank hopelessly to her knees.

James gave Mia a hug and put on a brave face as Alfie and Fleur wandered back down the beach. 'Never mind, another plane will come along soon. We can try again.'

'How come he didn't see us?' Fleur demanded with a burst of anger. 'He must have been blind!'

'Maybe he did see us.' Alfie clung to the last shred of hope. 'Think about it – he couldn't have landed anyway. A Cessna needs a landing strip of eight hundred metres. There's nothing like that amount of flat land on Dolphin Island.'

Fleur took this in. 'Trust you, Alfie,' she muttered.

'What?'

'To know techie stuff like that.'

'It's true, though. Where would he have landed?'

James nodded. 'You're right, son. And it is possible that he did see us then sent a message to someone on the mainland, giving our exact position.'

'So they could send a boat to fetch us?' Fleur's

spirits rose again. If this was true, they all needed to take their turn up at Lookout Point.

'It might take a while,' her dad warned. 'And it's best not to get our hopes up too high.'

Nevertheless, Alfie, Mia and Fleur set off at a run up the beach. They scrambled up the cliff path, past Butterfly Falls and on up to the ledge where they found their mum sitting cross-legged by the fire. By the time they arrived, they'd convinced themselves that a rescue boat was already on its way.

Katie was surprised to see the eager looks on their faces.

'Mum, we've come to help you keep a lookout.' Mia plonked herself down beside her and let her legs swing over the edge of the ledge. 'We're waiting for a boat.'

'You are, are you?' Katie looked up at Alfie and Fleur.

Fleur swallowed her last remaining doubts. 'Yes. The Cessna's pilot has probably sent a message to a coastguard on the mainland or a ship in the Torres Strait. Now they know where we are, it won't be long before they come to fetch us.'

Katie slowly nodded and made room for Alfie and Fleur on the ledge. 'Best not to get your hopes up though.'

'That's what Dad said.' Alfie frowned then gazed out to sea. He noticed a few wispy clouds – the sort that could quickly gather and be whipped up by the wind into a tropical storm. He wasn't worried about it though and for once he didn't even notice their three dolphins swimming close to the reef. His eyes were fixed far out to sea, searching for the tiny speck that would sail on to the horizon, navigating the treacherous currents between these remote islands. There was no doubt in his mind – rescue was close at hand.

Chapter Four

It rained hard during the night. Thunder woke Alfie from a deep sleep. It rumbled down the mountain and was followed by a fork of lightning that lit up the black sky. Then there was another sharp clap of thunder that woke the others in George's Cave, followed by a rush of wind and a loud crash that brought a startled Alfie, Fleur, Mia and James out into the open. A second bolt of lightning lit up a scene of fresh destruction as several tree trunks swayed then toppled on to the remains of their old camp site. *Crash* – another came down as the gale force gusts tore up the roots of the blackened trees.

Then the heavens opened and the rain came down. It lashed against the cliff face and threatened both their fires. Up at Lookout Point, Katie fought desperately to keep hers alight, piling it high with logs and branches. Torrential rain killed the flames with a loud hiss and within minutes she was left with only smouldering remains. Down at the foot of the cliff, the others worked as a team. Shoulders hunched against the wind, they formed a human chain between the log store and the campfire. James pulled a heavy piece of driftwood from the stack stored underneath an overhanging rock. He passed it to Fleur who handed it on to Mia who staggered under its weight before she passed it on to Alfie. He flung the wood on to the fire and watched the flames lick at it. He glanced upwards, praying for the rain to stop. Sharp drops stung his cheeks as, hardly able to see because of the smoke, he took another lump of wood from Mia and went on feeding the fire.

'More!' he cried as the storm raged on. Lightning flashed and thunder boomed. 'We have to keep it alight!'

They worked together – log after log and branch after branch until their store of firewood was almost gone. The thin tongues of flame flickered and hissed, almost died then flared up again, boosted by a wild, blustering wind that blasted a wall of heat towards Alfie. He was forced to take a quick step back and shield his face with his arm.

'I think the rain's stopping,' Fleur yelled at last through a cloud of swirling smoke.

Orange flames were driven this way and that, gaining strength as the storm eased. They lit up four anxious, smoke-blackened faces – eyes fixed on the fire that could mean the difference between life and death to the stranded family. A final flash of lightning forked through the air and thunder growled its farewell.

Alfie held out his palm. He felt only a light smattering of cold drops. Up on the cliff path, his mum had stopped for breath by Butterfly Falls, looking down at the group huddled together in the flickering light of the campfire. She came down and joined them, sighing and shaking her head over recent events – the Big Fire that had destroyed their camp, the plane that had flown over the island without changing course to take a closer look, and now, to cap it all, a tropical storm that had robbed them of their lookout fire.

'Luck has not been on our side lately,' Katie

murmured as they all sat around the fire waiting for the sky to lighten in the east.

Fleur frowned. It wasn't like her mum to sound downhearted. Normally Katie smiled her way through each day and made the best of things. 'It's not so bad. The storm didn't beat us – we've still got one fire.'

'So the rescue boat will be able to see our smoke,' Alfie pointed out. Like Mia and Fleur, he refused to let go of the thin thread of hope that at any moment a boat would appear on the horizon.

Their mum looked long and hard at their dad but said nothing.

Fleur backed Alfie up. 'Yes – as soon as it's light we can build the lookout fire again. Then the rescue boat definitely can't miss us.'

Mia shuffled sideways to sit closer to Katie. She placed her fingers around the smooth surface of her dolphin charm. 'See this, Mum? It's for good luck. The boat will come and get us – I know it will.'

*

Day 46 dawned with a clear sky. Rainwater trickled down the mountainside and formed fresh waterfalls on the cliff face. They splashed from ledge to ledge until they reached the beach then soaked into the sand.

Fleur's first job of the morning was to fill one of the new containers with fresh water – an easy job after the downpour of the night before. She climbed the cliff path to a chorus of croaking frogs hidden in the broad-leaved undergrowth and walked through clouds of blue butterflies, stopping only to identify a red bird with purple wings nesting in a bush high up on the cliff face. It was a female Eclectus parrot, she decided – with a beautiful black beak and yellow eyes. Taking care not to disturb her, she went a long way round to reach the main falls. As she held her container in position and the water gurgled into it, she glanced out to sea – *no boat, no dolphins, worse luck* – and then up the mountain to spy a bunch of macaques staring down at her.

'Hey,' she said out loud by way of greeting. She smiled broadly.

The monkeys approached warily on all fours, long tails waving and twitching, comical tufts of dark brown hair sticking up from the tops of their heads. A baby on its mother's back made Fleur sigh with pleasure – he had pink, pointy ears and a pink face with enormous dark eyes – *so-o-o cute!* Two bold youngsters ran ahead of the rest then squatted at the top of the waterfall, about three metres above her. When she moved to ease the weight of her rapidly filling container, they squealed and ran away.

Fleur laughed. She straightened up then screwed the top on her container as four adult monkeys appeared. 'Don't think you can follow me down to our new food store and rob us again,' she warned. 'You've caused us enough trouble already.'

They stared long and hard at the human intruder. Fleur tried to imagine what they must be thinking about her – that she had a mane of long brown hair but smooth, bare skin everywhere else. There was a white covering over her shoulders and chest (her T-shirt) and something blue beneath it (her shorts). Strange sounds came out of her mouth. A very odd creature – with fingers and thumbs like them but in other ways different. And how did she get by without a tail?

Still chuckling to herself, she carried the water

down the path, and by the time she reached the beach she was glad to see Alfie returning from his morning spent beachcombing on Echo Cave Beach.

'It's just you and me for lunch,' she told him as she met him by the new tyre swing. 'The others relit the lookout fire then headed south to cut more bamboo. They took dried fish and jackfruit with them.'

He nodded at her without smiling. In fact, he seemed more down in the dumps than he had been for ages.

'What's up?' she asked.

'No boat.' He muttered two short words and shoved his fists deep into his shorts pockets.

'Yeah – no, I know.' He didn't have to say any more. Hope was like flour passing through a sieve – the more you shook it, the quicker it fell through the holes. For the first time, Fleur began to fear the worst.

'I found this in Echo Cave.' Alfie drew out a black felt-tip. 'The top's watertight so I reckon it'll still work. And this.' He pulled out a crumpled blue armband – the kind that kids used when they learned how to swim. 'We can blow it up and use it for something – I don't know what.'

'A lilo for George,' Fleur suggested with a grin.

'Geckos don't like water. I mean – can they even swim?' Still muttering and frowning, Alfie decided to go for a quick dip and Fleur soon followed him. He waded into the water then launched himself into a breaking wave.

'Wait for me!' she called as she watched his head bob up through the white foam. Then she saw that they had a dolphin visitor – unmistakably Pearl, with her curved fin and wide, dark eyes.

'Wow!' she breathed, as Alfie's dolphin rose clear of the water. Pearl soared into the air and twisted then plunged back in, creating a rainbow spray by whacking her tail hard against the surface.

Alfie spun round in time to see Pearl jump. He spread his arms wide and waited for her to reappear.

Fleur swam to join him. 'Where are the others?' she gasped, scanning the horizon for another sighting. For a while she thought her eyes were playing tricks and that Stormy and Jazz must be hidden by the shimmering haze over the reef. Or perhaps they were teasing her in a game of hide-and-seek.

'Hey, Pearl!' Alfie yelled when she reappeared by the headland separating them from Turtle Beach. 'I'm over here.'

Pearl swam swiftly towards him with only the dome of her head visible above the surface. She clapped her jaws together then gave a series of chirps before swimming full circle around him.

'What's up?' he wondered out loud as she came close and nudged him towards the headland. 'Didn't you come to play?'

'More to the point, why aren't Jazz and Stormy with her?' Though Fleur was glad to see Pearl, it seemed odd that she was by herself. In fact, the more she thought about it, the stranger it seemed. 'Dolphins are meant to stick together,' she pointed out. 'You're not supposed to leave your pod.'

'She knows that.' Alfie sounded cross. In fact, like Fleur, he was puzzled and scared about the risk Pearl had taken. 'Is everything OK?' he murmured to Pearl, who was still nudging him and now brought her jaws together with a light clapping sound.

'For a start, it's dangerous.' Fleur went on trying to

work it out. 'What if there's a shark or an orca hanging around? That's why you shouldn't go off by yourself, you know; especially not before you're fully grown.'

Alfie's dolphin thrashed her tail up and down then swam ahead towards the headland. 'Maybe she wants us to follow?' he suggested. 'Yeah, that's it – Stormy and Jazz must be waiting for us in Turtle Bay!'

That would solve the mystery, Fleur realized with a sigh of relief. But then again, why had they let Pearl come on ahead of them in the first place? There was only one way to find out, and Alfie was about to beat her to it because he'd already set off at a fast front crawl towards the headland. 'Wait for me!' she yelled as the force of the incoming tide swept her close to the rocks. She kicked hard and swam on through the breaking waves.

Pearl was waiting for Alfie and Fleur in the shallow water of Turtle Bay. There was still no sign of Jazz and Stormy and she went on signalling to them with loud clicks and agitated flicks of her flat tail flukes.

'Do you think she got separated from the pod by mistake?' Alfie asked.

Fleur shook her head. 'Dolphins keep in touch by echolocation. They pick up tiny sound signals to stay close together. In other words, they never get lost or separated.'

'Yeah – I already know that,' he said with a frown. He was growing convinced that Pearl had deliberately separated herself from the pod and paid them this visit to deliver a warning. 'So she's here on purpose and she's trying to tell us something.'

'If that's true, she must know it's safer for us to wait here at Turtle Beach than in Base Camp Bay,' Fleur pointed out.

Alfie and Fleur trod water and watched the young dolphin, who gave her birdlike whistle as she swam to the shore and almost stranded herself on the beach.

Alfie's heart skipped. 'Don't do that! Come back!' he yelled.

The next wave refloated Pearl and she turned and swam towards them then nudged them from behind, like a sheepdog herding sheep.

'She's telling us to get out of the water,' Fleur realized.

So they obeyed her and waded on to the beach.

'What now?' Alfie asked. Feeling even more uneasy, he scanned the horizon. He could still see the reef off Base Camp Bay and to the south there was the headland separating them from Pirate Cave Beach. There was no wind and the sea was calm. If the rest of Pearl's pod was anywhere near, they would be easily spotted.

'Maybe Pearl is sick.' Fleur didn't intend to worry Alfie by voicing her latest fear but it slipped out anyway.

Now his heart started to race. 'How do you mean – sick?'

'Or scared,' Fleur continued quickly. She too searched the horizon.

'What of?' Alfie whispered.

The sun shone down fiercely; the waves crashed against the rocks then rolled towards the shore. A hundred metres out to sea, Pearl swam in slow circles, keeping watch.

Chapter Five

'It's hot. We should find somewhere to shelter,' Fleur told Alfie.

The fierce sun was at its highest point. There was no shade at the water's edge and they weren't wearing hats.

'I'm not leaving until I know Pearl's OK,' he muttered. He scrunched up his eyes and peered out through his long lashes, his blurred gaze fixed on his faithful dolphin friend.

Fleur studied her brother's anxious face then glanced out to sea. Pearl still patrolled the bay. 'How do we make her leave?'

He ignored Fleur's question. 'What if she is sick like you said? How do we help her?'

Fleur didn't know the answer. Silently she urged

Pearl to swim away to rejoin her pod. 'Lend me your whistle. I want to try signalling to her.'

Alfie drew the whistle from his pocket and handed it over.

Placing it between her lips, Fleur strode into the sea.

Pearl noticed her and cut rapidly through the water to drive her back on to dry land.

Almost losing her balance as Pearl brushed against her, Fleur gave a shrill blast on the whistle.

Pearl opened her jaws and gave Fleur a close-up view of the inside of her cavernous mouth with its neat rows of small, rounded teeth. She clapped it shut then nudged Fleur out of the water, letting the waves break over her head and waiting until Fleur was back on dry land before turning tail and swimming clear of the shore.

'She doesn't *look* sick,' Alfie said uncertainly. Pearl's movements were as fast and agile as ever. Her eyes were bright. Still, his stomach tied itself into a tight knot as he tried to work out what was happening.

Fleur gave the whistle back to him. 'Well, that didn't

work out too well,' she muttered. She raised her arms and made a shooing motion. 'Go away, Pearl!' she yelled. It made no difference – Alfie's dolphin refused to end her patrol.

After a few more minutes of watching and wondering, it was Alfie who finally turned to Fleur and spoke the dreaded words. 'Listen, we both know what this is about – it's the tiger shark. Pearl's here to tell us that we're safer sitting it out here than in Base Camp Bay. The problem is, she took a great big risk to keep us out of danger and now she's cut herself off from her pod.'

'You mean, even though we can't see the shark, it's lurking off our bay and it's now too dangerous for Pearl to leave?' Fleur's stomach churned as Alfie's words sank in.

He nodded. 'And no way can we go into the water to help her – she wouldn't let us. The thing is, Fleur … the shark that was here before has definitely, one hundred per cent certain, come back!'

*

Alfie stayed with Pearl all through the baking hot

56

afternoon. He sent Fleur to tell the others what was happening.

'What *is* happening?' she asked before she left.

His answer was short and spoken through gritted teeth. 'You know!'

Fleur shook her head. 'We're only guessing,' she argued. 'We haven't actually seen the shark.'

'Go and tell them,' he insisted. A deep frown creased his forehead as he found a place to sit. He chose a crevice in the rock on the Turtle Beach headland that provided a good viewing spot for him to look out to sea. He drew his knees up to his chin and wrapped his arms around his legs, hunkering down for a long vigil.

Reluctantly Fleur said goodbye then walked back to Base Camp Bay. There was no sign of anyone – the site of the shelter was silent and still, apart from a brightly coloured gecko that scuttled across the newly completed platform and a tree kangaroo high in a palm tree that had survived the Big Fire. It clung to the trunk with its strong forearms and gazed down at Fleur with intense curiosity.

She tried to figure out where her mum and dad and

Mia would be. At this time of day they usually kept out of the heat so it was unlikely that they'd be beachcombing or fishing. Perhaps they would be sheltering in the shade of the overhanging rock at Lookout Point. Fleur headed up the cliff path. She stopped often to look down into the bay where she could see Pearl swimming a couple of hundred metres out from the shore, patrolling steadily between the two headlands, and Alfie in his white T-shirt and red shorts squatting in the rocky crevice. Each time she checked, she felt her heart skip a beat and she had to take a deep breath then force herself to go on.

By the time she'd paused at Butterfly Falls to take a long drink then finally reached the lookout fire, she was exhausted. She had to wipe away the sweat that trickled from her forehead into her eyes. And there was no one here after all. The recently fed fire burned steadily. Smoke gathered under the overhang before being carried away on the breeze. One more glance from this high vantage point down into the neighbouring bay told her that everything was still the same – Pearl swam steadily to and fro, Alfie squatted on the rock and, thank heavens, there was no sign of the feared enemy, the killer shark.

Where next? Fleur glanced up at the mountain peak behind her. A few hundred metres of steeply sloping scrubland separated her from the edge of the forest. All the bushes had been scorched in the recent blaze and there was a covering of grey ash over the rocks and gravel. Then, about fifty metres from where the trees began, there were green shrubs that the flames hadn't touched and beyond that the thick canopy of trees and creepers that she dreaded. Then she spotted her dad's sweatshirt hanging from a low branch of a jackfruit tree. *I bet that's where the others are, she decided. They've gone to collect more firewood and I'll have to go in after them.*

With her heart thudding against her ribs, she went on. She was short of breath and her throat was dry. What if the hissing, lumbering creature that she'd heard but not seen was lying in wait? What if her mum, dad and Mia weren't there after all and she was walking straight into the predator's trap? It was definitely a hunter because she'd seen the wild boar family fleeing from it. That meant it was a meat eater, a carnivore. And as if she needed reminding of this fact, she passed close to where she and Alfie had found some pig bones and a skull, noticing a scattering of scorched ribs and leg bones still lying in the dirt.

Alfie's right – no animal would stick around on this side of the island after the fire. It must have crossed over to the west. Fleur repeated this thought to herself as she approached the edge of the forest. She came to her dad's sweatshirt and the thick, smooth trunks of two jackfruit trees rising high above her head. Clusters of big yellow fruits the size of footballs were visible through the broad green leaves, and ripe, rotting ones lay on the ground surrounded by swarms of wasps. She skirted wide of the buzzing insects and stepped fearfully into the shade of the forest.

Once out of the blinding sunlight, her eyes took time to adjust. 'Dad?' she called into the deep, cool shadows. 'Mum? Mia?'

There was no answer. She brushed against a low-hanging creeper and shrank back, trying not to breathe in the dank smell of mud and decaying leaves. She could see better now – well enough to find her footing and edge along a fallen tree trunk towards a lighter area where the canopy of leaves was not so thick. 'Is anybody here?' she called again, every nerve tingling with fear.

'Boo!' Mia sprang out from behind a tree.

Fleur let out a yelp then a groan. 'Don't do that!'

'It's only me!' A laughing Mia danced towards her, her face a pale disc in the dappled light. 'I wanted to make you jump.'

'Well you did.' Fleur's anger quickly vanished. No one could stay mad at Mia for long and anyway Fleur was relieved to find her.

'Mum and Dad are collecting wood. They're just over there, in the clearing. Come on!'

Steering clear of the oozing mud, they slowly made their way to where James and Katie stockpiled fuel for the fires. Katie took one look at Fleur's serious expression and knew at once that something was wrong.

'Hi, Fleury – what is it?'

The whole story came rushing out – how Pearl had

shown up in Base Camp Bay alone, how she'd refused to go away and rejoin her pod, how Alfie was convinced that she'd come to warn him about the tiger shark.

The word 'shark' made James put down the branch he'd been dragging. He frowned then scratched at his beard. 'What do you think, Fleur? Is Alfie right?'

'I don't know – probably. We're worried about Pearl. If the shark is cruising around offshore, she shouldn't be separated from the others.'

'You mean, how is she going to rejoin them?' he prompted.

Fleur nodded. 'She doesn't stand a chance if the shark attacks.'

The smile vanished from Mia's face. She looked fearfully from her dad to her mum.

'OK, let's down tools,' Katie decided. 'We're out of here.'

She led the way along the track they'd made for themselves, out into the glaring light. The little family group spread out across the open scrubland then came together again at Lookout Point.

'See.' Fleur pointed to the tiny figure of Alfie on the

headland, still as a statue as he kept watch. For a few moments she couldn't spot Pearl but then she saw her rise to the surface and spout water through her blowhole. 'They're still there,' she murmured.

'Try not to worry too much.' James took over the lead down the cliff path. 'Pearl's a smart dolphin – she knows how to stay out of the shark's way.'

'But she's young,' Fleur pointed out. 'Under two metres long and a tiger shark is much, much bigger.' Bigger and stronger, with teeth that sliced through flesh, its small eyes set well back in its terrifying, wedge-shaped head. A scavenger with 360-degree vision, and a ruthless killer.

They came to the bottom of the cliff and hurried on past building materials that had been gathered for the new shelter – a stack of palm fronds waiting to be woven into wall panels beside sturdy bamboo canes – on past the half-finished canoe and the new food store, down the beach past George's Cave and on towards the headland where Alfie kept watch.

At last they reached him and gathered around.

'Well?' Katie asked, pushing her hair back from her face. 'Any sign of the shark?'

Alfie shook his head. After so long looking at the sea and sitting in the heat, he felt dizzy and faint. The blue horizon seemed to tilt and the roar of the breaking waves drowned out all other sounds.

Fleur followed Pearl's progress from one side of the bay to the other. 'She can't stay here for ever,' she murmured.

'Neither can we,' James said in a quiet, kind voice. 'At some point we have to go back to camp and leave her to it.'

'No.' Alfie's face was set in stubborn lines. 'I'm not leaving.' Pearl had risked her life to come and warn them and now it was up to him to stick it out until he was sure she was safe.

Katie sat down next to him. 'Alfie, I'm thinking ahead. What happens when it gets dark?'

'I'll stay here.'

'And what if we have another storm?'

'I'll still stay.'

She looked at the face peering out from under the

brim of the hat she'd just given him. Alfie's mouth was pursed, his brown eyes scrunched into a determined expression. 'OK,' she agreed. 'I'll wait here with you.'

James turned to Fleur and Mia and tried to lighten the mood. 'Come on, you two – let's go back for food and water for these two crazy people.'

'You can have smoked fish,' Mia suggested. 'And sugarcane. Yum!'

'OK.' With one last glance at Pearl, Fleur agreed. She looked again – and a third time. There was a fin in the water, out beyond the reef, disappearing under the waves and then resurfacing on the near side of the rocks. She closed her eyes and clenched her fists, then without saying a word, she forced herself to look for a fourth time.

The lone fin approached Turtle Bay. Was it a shark's long, pointed fin or the curved dorsal fin of a dolphin? What shape was the tail as it thrashed through the water – did it have the dangerous, pointed upper fluke of a predator, or the flat, broad tail of a dolphin that would signal that all was well?

Alfie followed Fleur's gaze. His heart thudded as he

spotted the indistinct fin. As it drew nearer, Pearl sensed its approach and retreated close to the headland where the Fisher family had gathered.

Curved! A curved fin! An adult dolphin swam to join Pearl, followed by others racing to catch up, rising out of the ocean in great, athletic arcs, surging through the foaming water that broke against the reef, cutting cleanly through the smooth, calm waters of Turtle Bay. Soon there were fifteen or so sleek grey creatures, swimming together in search of their wandering youngster. They clicked and whistled, calling out for her to return.

'It's Marina.' Relief flooded through Alfie's body and he stood up for a better view of what happened next.

Marina was Pearl's mother. He recognized her short, blunt nostrum – her under-jaw – and her large, bright eyes. He watched as she swam between him and Pearl, rounding up her daughter and ushering her out to join the waiting pod. The others circled her, giving welcoming yelps and slapping their tails on the water as the worried mother gave Pearl a strong flick with her tail flukes then nudged her towards the reef and the open sea beyond.

'Marina's telling her off,' Fleur realized. Just like any mother would whose youngster had wandered off without asking permission. She felt a surge of joy as she witnessed the reunion.

'Happy now?' Katie asked Alfie, who hovered on the tip of the headland as if eager to dive in and join the dolphins. She took hold of his hand and drew him back.

It was as if there'd been a storm inside his head and now the skies were clearing. The sun was coming out. 'Yeah – cool,' he sighed.

Pearl had reached the horizon. She leaped clear of the surface, twisted and turned in the air, then re-entered the water and swam on with Marina and the others. Yes, the shark might be back in the area, lurking in shallow waters and waiting to seize its prey. But Pearl was with her pod. She was safe.

Chapter Six

'No peace for the wicked.' James sighed as he and Katie put on their straw hats and went fishing for supper. They took with them a fishing net made from interwoven palm fronds tied to a bamboo hoop and attached to a long pole.

'What did Dad mean?' Mia asked Alfie, who was laying out bamboo canes and cutting them to the same length. She swung high on the tyre swing, to and fro with strong kicks of her legs.

'He meant we always have jobs to do.' A knot of concentration creased his brow.

'So we're not really wicked?' Grown-ups sometimes came out with sentences that confused her.

'No way!' Fleur came up behind and caught hold of the swing.

'Whoa!' Mia hung in midair. 'Let go, Fleury.'

'Only if you promise to stop pestering Alfie with questions.' Fleur's job for the evening was to climb the cliff and look for birds' eggs for breakfast, but first she wanted to have fun with Mia. 'Promise?'

'I promise. Now, let go!'

Fleur released the swing. 'Hold on tight,' she instructed.

'Whee! Push me higher.' A breeze lifted Mia's mop of brown hair from her sticky forehead.

'Please?' Fleur reminded her.

'Pretty please!' Mia loved the new swing – it was like flying and she felt like Wonder Woman after all.

Fleur pushed for a while and chatted with Alfie. 'What are the canes for?'

'To make frames for the shelter walls,' he explained as he laid them out to form big squares then started to bind the corners together with rope. 'You're better at weaving than me, so you can start work with the palm fronds whenever you like.'

'After I've collected eggs.' Judging by the sun's position in the sky, they only had a couple of hours of daylight left. 'Are you coming with me, Mi-mi?'

'Nope.' Mia was happy to carry on swinging so Fleur went off alone. She climbed the path up to the falls then branched to her right, towards a ledge spattered with white gannet droppings – a sign that the big grey seabirds had made nests and laid eggs there. There was a sheer drop of about five metres below the ledge but Fleur was agile and not scared of heights. Working out safe footholds, she edged her way forwards and, sure enough, found five decent-sized eggs in a nest made of twigs and downy feathers. She took a bowl made from a coconut shell from the plastic sack hitched over one shoulder and put three of the eggs into it, leaving two for the hen bird to carry on hatching.

So far, so good. Fleur placed the eggs in the sack. *But we need more.* She glanced up and worked out where the next nest might be.

Down below, Mia complained to Alfie of a stomach ache.

'Better get off the swing then,' he advised.

So she jumped down with a whoop then bombarded him with more questions. 'What's that for?' 'How long

will it take to finish the new shelter?' 'When's supper?'
'When will Fleur be back?'

'For the walls.' 'Don't ask me.' 'After Mum and Dad
catch some fish.' 'Soon.' He answered without breaking
off from his task. The frames seemed sturdy so he
was happy.

'Is there really a tiger shark out there?' Mia asked as
she sat cross-legged in the sand.

Alfie stopped what he was doing and sat down
beside her. 'Yes, I'm pretty sure there is. We can rely
on Pearl to know when there's danger close by and
I figure a shark is the only reason she'd do what she
did earlier.'

'But she's OK?' A dark shadow appeared in Mia's
light brown eyes.

'She's fine, Mi-mi. So are Jazz and Stormy. As long as
the pod sticks together, the adults will look after the
young ones. But, remember, we've got a strict rule – we
all have to stay out of the water until the coast is clear.
No swimming.'

'When will we know that it's safe?'

'When Mum and Dad tell us it is.' He came up with

the best answer he could think of. Since they'd been on Dolphin Island he'd learned a lot about tiger sharks, mostly from Fleur. She'd told him how they hunted mostly at night and preyed on fish and birds, squid and turtles – whatever they could catch in their fearful jaws, including dolphins. They were restless, solo wanderers of the central Pacific Ocean, up to five metres long, lurking amongst wafting sea grass and fragile coral reefs close to the shore. They swam slowly until they spied their prey then put on a lethal burst of speed and made their kill. He kept all this from Mia as they sat on the beach and chatted. 'It'll probably be like the last time we got a shark visit – we'll be OK to swim after a few days at most.'

'Cool.' Mia smiled, rolled on to her stomach then rested her chin in her hands and changed the subject. 'So when will the boat come?'

This time Alfie couldn't disguise his feelings and he let out an unhappy sigh. By his reckoning it was thirty-six hours since the Cessna had flown over the island. And with every hour that passed his hopes had sunk further until they'd reached rock bottom. 'Maybe it won't,' he said quietly, watching his little sister's face fall once more. 'Honestly – we can't actually tell if the pilot and passengers saw us, can we?'

'But you said they did!'

'We *hoped* they did,' he reminded her. What was the point of pretending any longer?

'So they didn't see our "HELP" sign or our smoke?' The truth dawned on Mia and tears followed soon after.

'Maybe not,' he admitted in an even quieter voice.

She stood up and started to walk slowly down the beach.

'Where are you going?' Alfie called after her.

'To George's Cave,' she replied in a small, trembling voice. 'To fetch Monkey.'

*

That night sleep wouldn't come to Fleur. As the others drifted off in their own corners of George's Cave, she tossed and turned on her woven mat, eyes wide open and listening to the restless waves break on the shore. She tried counting – not sheep but bright green geckos sitting in a row on a sunny rock – one, two, three, four, five …

She reached thirty and was still wide awake, with twitchy legs and a dry mouth. *Try something else.* How many species of butterfly did she know? Red Admiral, Monarch, Blue Moon, Large Tiger – she began her list but soon her attention wandered to dolphin facts. An adult dolphin had between eighteen and twenty-six pairs of teeth. The maximum time a dolphin could stay underwater without coming up for air was seven minutes. Each dolphin had a signature whistle,

different from any other dolphin's. They never slept –
instead they rested one side of their brain while the
other stayed alert and awake.

I'm like a dolphin, a sleepless Fleur realized, *only I
can't split my brain into two and be awake and asleep
at the same time.*

Eventually, after what felt like hours and hours, she
did drift off. But she dreamed as she slept of the hissing
hunter that lived in the forest on the mountain. She

pictured teeth as sharp as a lion's, capable of tearing flesh from bones, and jaws with a grip as strong as a killer whale's. Then she heard the monster's heavy, lumbering tread as it emerged from the jungle at midnight, and she fled in her nightmare down the mountain slope, past Lookout Point and Butterfly Falls, scrambling down the cliff without looking round but hearing the creature in hot pursuit – heavy and hissing, opening its jaws. She ran across the beach. It gained on her. She clambered up on to the headland then dived into the sea.

Waves closed over her head but for the moment she was safe. She swam in warm currents among black rocks with shoals of silversides. Then sea grass wrapped itself around her arms and legs and held her underwater while an enormous creature swam slowly towards her – its back was a dull blue, its belly whitish-yellow, with dark stripes down its flanks. The tiger shark opened its jaws and kept on coming …

*

Fleur woke covered in sweat and gasping for air. Outside the cave, a grey light crept over the horizon, soon followed by faint pink. Thank heavens it was morning and her nightmare visions would fade with the rising sun. Fleur marked Day 47 with a new notch on the calendar stick. Forty-seven days equalled almost seven long weeks of scorching heat broken up by thunderstorms and torrential rain, seven weeks of baking in the blazing sun's rays then watching clouds roll in and lightning split the stormy sky. Cast adrift on Dolphin Island, the Fisher family had found shelter, built fires and survived all that Nature could throw at them.

Thanks to the dolphins, Fleur realized as she yawned and stretched then scanned the empty horizon. *We'd never have done it without them.*

Mia emerged from the cave with Monkey tucked under her arm. Her hair was tousled and her eyelids still heavy with sleep. 'Hey, I wanted to do the calendar stick,' she complained.

'Sorry, I forgot.' Lack of sleep made Fleur more offhand than usual and she set off towards the campfire without inviting Mia to come along.

'Wait for me!' Mia trotted after her. When she saw

that their dad had already started to make breakfast, she overtook Fleur with a slap of her thigh, yelling 'giddy-up!' as she broke into a gallop.

Back at the cave, Alfie woke up to find Katie still sleeping soundly. His stomach felt hollow – it was time to eat. After breakfast there would be the usual chores – collecting water and firewood, coconuts and jackfruit. Then the more interesting stuff: beachcombing on Pirate Cave Beach and, if he was lucky, getting as far as Black Crab Cove and back home before sunset.

Katie turned over in her sleep as Alfie crept out into the open then followed Fleur and Mia up the beach. He was excited by the idea of reaching the cove and exploring the wreck of *Dolphin* again. The old sailing ship had rested in sand dunes for a couple of centuries, a ghostly reminder of sailors who had navigated by starlight. During the day, a lad of his own age would have been sent to climb the mast and perch in the crow's nest, using a telescope to spy dangers ahead – rocky coastlines or pirate ships, or perhaps an approaching storm.

'Hey, Alfie.' Mia greeted him with her mouth full of scrambled eggs.

'Hey.' He used his fingers to scoop up egg from the metal plate that had been rescued from the ashes after the Big Fire. They'd found the plate in a cobwebby old chest that he and Fleur had found inside *Dolphin*. They'd carried it back and used it as a frying pan for fish and eggs.

'Good?' James asked as he watched Alfie gobble down his breakfast.

He nodded. 'Does anyone want to come with me to Black Crab Cove later? We can check out the wreck again.'

'Me!' Mia drank water from a coconut shell then wiped her mouth with the back of her hand.

'Fleur?' Alfie inquired.

'I don't know. Maybe.' *What's the point?* she thought. *We've already brought back everything useful from the old ship. Besides, there was a snake there. If we go back, we run the risk of being bitten by a poisonous reptile.*

'That's not like you,' James remarked. 'Who knows

what new species of flora and fauna you might come across?'

'Skinks, flying foxes, possums.' Alfie did his best to tempt her. 'We haven't seen any of those on the island so far but they're probably around if we look hard enough.'

'Anyway, we can't go swimming and we won't see our dolphins.' Mia reminded them all of the danger that lurked offshore. 'That means we have to explore instead.'

'We could stay here and draw a new map with the felt-tip that Alfie found.' For once, Fleur resisted the lure of the island's wildlife. 'We can make up new names.'

'Boring,' Mia said with a frown.

Alfie took the pen out of his pocket and scribbled on the back of his hand to make sure that it worked. 'No, it's a cool idea. We can draw it on a piece of canvas like last time.'

Fleur looked ahead to a quiet, relaxing afternoon. 'We'll sit in the shade on Turtle Beach.'

'Cool. You can draw the outline.' Alfie knew that

Fleur was a better artist than him. 'But Mia and I get to choose some new names.'

'It looks like Black Crab Cove will have to wait,' James told his youngest daughter. 'Anyway, it's probably just as well to stay closer to home while there's a chance that there's a tiger shark hanging around.'

Mia gave a long, loud sigh. *No swimming and no exploring. Hardly any fun. Just a day doing jobs and making a boring old map.*

Chapter Seven

'We've got walls but still no roof.' Alfie and Fleur's hard work on Day 47 had paid off and by the time the sun had reached its height the new shelter was beginning to take shape. There were steps up to the platform and four woven panels in place, with several long, straight branches piled at the foot of the cliff, waiting to be used as timber for the roof.

'We'll start on that tomorrow.' Armed with a length of bamboo, Alfie eagerly took the lead. 'Now it's time for some R and R.'

'What's that?' Mia trod in his footsteps in the soft sand. Alfie's legs were longer than hers so she had to take giant strides.

'Rest and relaxation,' Fleur replied. It was map-making time so they were heading for Turtle Beach where Alfie kept his small stash of canvas. She was happy to let him take the lead and allow her mind to drift while Mia chattered on.

'But I don't want to rest. I want to make a map.'

'You've changed your tune,' he grunted.

'A *map*, not a *nap*, eh?' Fleur smiled then pulled Mia away from a jellyfish stranded in a shallow pool at the edge of the rocks. 'Well, you're in luck, because that's exactly what we're going to do.'

'Map time – yay!' Tugging free, Mia scrambled over the headland to catch up with her brother. She followed him to the crevice in the rocks where the canvas was safely stored.

He took it out, laid it flat then cut out a rectangular piece with his knife, rolled up the rest of the canvas and put it back in the niche before letting Fleur choose a breezy spot close to the bamboo grove at the edge of the beach. Soon they were all sitting down and Fleur used Alfie's pen to sketch an outline in the shape of an upside-down teardrop.

'This is the north and this is the south,' she explained to Mia. 'The west is over here, to the left, and the east coast is on the right. We know more about the east side because here's where we've set up camp. Here's Base Camp Bay.' Marking the spot about a third of the way from the northern point of the island, she then went inland a little way to mark Lookout Point.

'And this is Turtle Beach.' Alfie leaned over Fleur's shoulder and pointed. 'What comes next, Mi-mi, after Turtle Beach?'

'Pirate Cave Beach and then Black Crab Cove.' Pleased that she knew the answer, Mia gabbled on faster than Fleur could write. 'That's where we found the *Dolphin* wreck, and then there's an amazing arch-thingy in the rock.'

'An amazing arch-thingy?' Alfie echoed.

'Yes – you know. A rock that comes high over your head and you can swim under it to the next beach.'

Fleur sat with her pen poised. 'What shall we call that then?'

'How about Magic Arch 'cos we don't know how it was made – so it's like magic? And you have to put the mountain in. Call it Mystery Mountain.'

'Slow down,' Fleur pleaded. She wrote down Mia's

first idea carefully and neatly. "M-a-ǧ-i-c A-r-c-h."

'And now Mystery Mountain.'

Alfie gave a quick nod. 'Good name, Mi-mi – especially since we don't know much about what lives up there.'

Fleur finished writing then sat back. 'Do you want to draw a nice picture and write "Dolphin Island", here in the space at the top?' she asked Mia.

Mia seized the pen and concentrated hard. She wrote carefully then took off her lucky charm to copy its shape, drawing three dolphins over the top of the words. 'This one is Pearl, this is Jazz and this is Stormy,' she said proudly.

'Cool,' Alfie and Fleur said together. A three-dolphin emblem was exactly right for their map, which they finished off with Mangrove Bay and Land's End to the south and Echo Cave Beach to the north.

'So can we go and explore the wreck later?' Mia asked as they rolled up the map then prepared to make their way back to Base Camp Bay.

'I don't see why not.' Fleur felt her sense of curiosity return and now she was open to adventure. She climbed the headland then paused to look out towards the reef. 'Hey, guess who?' she cried as she pointed to the familiar shape of Jazz tail-walking his way towards them. He was the most acrobatic of their three young dolphin friends and she felt proud of the way he seemed to dance across the water towards them.

'Jazz!' Mia yelled with delight and waved both hands. 'And Stormy! Hi, Stormy! We're over here, on the rocks!'

Mia's very own dolphin surged ahead of Jazz, slicing cleanly through the water with only his head and dorsal fin visible. He made a beeline for her, then as soon as he reached her, he swiftly turned tail. As he swam back towards Jazz, Fleur's dolphin plunged gracefully out of sight.

Alfie kept his gaze fixed on the reef. He shaded his eyes with his hands, expecting to see Pearl's curved fin appear any second, in Stormy and Jazz's frothy wake.

'What's up?' Fleur wondered. Jazz and Stormy approached slowly this time until they came to within a few metres of the rocks. They made high-pitched, abrupt noises that sounded more like yelps than whistles, looking up at Fleur, Alfie and Mia and clapping their jaws together in an agitated way.

'Yes, what's wrong – where's Pearl?' Mia voiced the question that neither of the others dared speak.

Oh no – not again. Alfie felt his stomach tighten as he gazed out across the bay.

'Don't worry – she's probably fishing with Marina and the others.' Fleur's shaky voice showed that she didn't believe what she said. Besides, she had to fight hard to resist the urge to dive in to join Jazz and Stormy. 'No, we can't go in the water,' she reminded Mia, who also teetered at the edge of the rocks.

Alfie shook his head. 'No, Fleur – Pearl's not busy fishing. If she knew that Stormy and Jazz had come to Base Camp Bay and if everything was normal, she'd be here with them.'

'Maybe she's playing hide-and-seek.' Mia scrambled over the rocks then jumped down on to the sand. She paddled knee-deep into the water and peered under an overhang where the waves churned and white, frothing eddies whirled out the far side.

Fleur went to fetch her and drag her back to the

beach. Meanwhile, Jazz and Stormy stayed close to Alfie and went on swimming in tight circles.

The effort of pulling Mia back on to dry land made Fleur breathless. 'Did you see anything under there?'

'No,' Mia confessed.

'Where are you, Pearl?' Alfie muttered from the vantage point of the headland. 'Please show us that you're OK.'

He stared out towards the reef and for a few moments he felt a burst of relief loosen the knot in his stomach when he saw five more dolphins enter the bay. They were led by Marina and swam speedily to join Stormy and Jazz. Any second now he would spot Pearl's curved fin and be able to make out the pinkish, pearly sheen of her belly.

As Marina neared the shore, she was overtaken by the four other adult dolphins. They surrounded Stormy and Jazz then started to herd the youngsters around the headland. To keep them in their sights, Fleur and Mia would have to rejoin Alfie on the rocks.

'Why are they shooing Stormy and Jazz away?' Mia asked as she scrambled up. She glanced at Alfie and saw that his eyes were dark with worry.

'Because they know the shark's still around.' Fleur realized this was the only possible explanation. At this rate, it wouldn't only be Mia who she had to hold back – now Alfie looked as if he was about to take a headlong dive into the water. She grabbed his wrist and pulled him away from the edge.

Meanwhile, the four adult dolphins thrashed their tails against the water and forced Jazz and Stormy away from the shore. In an effort to resist, the two youngsters leaped clear of the water and out of the circle of dolphins that had formed around them. The adults quickly corralled them again and pushed them further out to sea.

'Let go!' Alfie tried to break free from Fleur. He didn't care how dangerous it was – this time he had to answer Stormy and Jazz's call to help them find Pearl. He used all his strength to pull away from Fleur and before she could stop him, he broke into a run then plunged into the breaking waves.

Fleur's heart almost stopped as she watched him dive underwater. Then his dark head resurfaced and he struck out in a clumsy front crawl, trying to catch up with the departing dolphins.

'Alfie, come back!' Even Mia could see that he would never be able to do it. Dolphins could swim way faster than people. 'Anyway, you're not allowed in the water!'

Luckily, Marina had stayed behind while members of the pod had rounded up Stormy and Jazz. She'd swum close to the headland, watching Alfie dive in, and now she went after him, diving underwater then resurfacing ahead of him so that she blocked his way forward. Then she used her beak to push him back towards Base Camp Bay. At three metres long and with two hundred kilograms of muscle behind her, she easily forced him to return to Fleur and Mia.

'Please!' he pleaded, as Marina nudged him ashore. 'I need to go with the pod – I have to help you find Pearl!'

'It's no good – Marina won't let you.' Fleur stooped to hitch her hands under Alfie's armpits and drag him on to the beach. His hair was plastered close to his skull, his legs and arms covered in wet sand.

Marina watched Fleur hold Alfie back. She swished her tail to change direction, steered out to sea then turned to make sure that he wasn't trying to follow her. By this time, the rest of the pod had swum beyond the reef and were out of sight.

'Go!' Every second that Marina stayed, the more danger she was in. Fleur swallowed hard. She felt like a traitor to Alfie, but Pearl's mother absolutely had to leave. 'Go!' she said again.

With one last, lingering look from her dark, bright eyes, Marina turned away. For her, the fastest way out of the bay was underwater so she dipped out of sight. One minute, two minutes, three minutes went by. The azure sea sparkled around the crescent of dark rocks that formed the reef. Meanwhile, Pearl's mother rejoined her pod.

Chapter Eight

'Missing!' The word lodged itself in Alfie's brain. Pearl was nowhere to be seen. He sat on the beach, slumped forward, biting his bottom lip and trying not to cry.

Missing. Missing. Missing.

Fleur scanned the horizon in vain as she tried to figure things out. *For some reason Pearl has been separated from Stormy and Jazz. They've looked everywhere for her – among the coral reefs, under overhanging rocks close to the shore. They've swum amongst dense sea grass, in and out of underwater caves, hoping to find her safe and well. But there's been no sign of her, so Stormy and Jazz did the only thing they could think of – they came to us to ask for help.*

'What are we going to do?' Mia whispered.

Alfie closed his eyes. He swallowed hard then stood

up. 'We're going to find Pearl.'

'How?' Mia ran after him as he strode towards base camp.

'Alfie, slow down.' Fleur caught up with him before Mia. 'Mia's right. How are we going to find Pearl if we're not allowed to go in the water?'

He answered quickly. 'For a start, me and you – we can hike along the coast for the rest of the day, searching in all the inlets. There are hundreds of places she could be hiding, keeping out of the shark's way until the coast is clear.'

'OK, good idea.' Fleur was doubtful but she agreed in order to keep Alfie happy. 'Mia, you have to run up to Lookout Point and tell Dad and Mum what's happening. Then stay there with them, OK?'

Mia's face crumpled. 'Let me come with you,' she pleaded.

'No, Mi-mi. Your job is important. You have to explain to them and stop them worrying about us. Tell them we promise not to go in the water.'

'When will you be back?'

'Before it gets dark.' Fleur sent Mia on her way,

noticing how young and small she looked in her grass skirt and straw hat as she climbed the cliff path. 'We'll need water,' she reminded Alfie, who had found their dad's neckerchief and tied it around his head to protect himself from the sun. 'And something to eat.' She packed two full water bottles, a coconut and some dried fish into a plastic bag, slinging it around her shoulder like a school satchel. 'Which way shall we head?' she asked when she was ready.

'South.' Alfie didn't waste time on words. With his knife tucked into his waistband, he set off across the beach towards the Turtle Bay headland.

The reflections of the midday sun's rays on the waves dazzled him, making it hard to see.

Fleur followed close behind and they soon reached the spot where Stormy and Jazz had come to ask for help. Now though, there were no dolphins off the rocky headland – just empty, glittering sea. 'What happens if we do find Pearl?' she wanted to know. 'What then?'

He had no answer to this so he jumped down on to Turtle Beach without speaking. He jogged on in the blazing heat, only slowing down to pick his way over the rocks of the next headland that separated them from Pirate Cave Beach. The rough surface hurt the soles of his feet but he took no notice as he stared beyond the breaking waves, down into the green depths of the ocean.

Fleur caught up with him once more. 'Anything?' she asked.

He shook his head. He'd spotted shoals of tiny silversides and a cluster of jellyfish close to the surface, even a big tarpon easing its way out from under a ledge. But Pearl was the only sea creature he was interested in.

'Here – have some water.' She handed him a bottle and watched him gulp it down. 'Not too much. We have to make it last.'

Alfie gave her the bottle back. He glanced up the beach and saw from the seaweed and driftwood debris left by the high tide that the water never reached the cave that gave this beach its name. He'd been inside it once with Mia, who had wriggled ahead of him through the low entrance, hoping to find a chest full of treasure. Of course, the cave had held nothing but broken shells and dried seaweed blown in by the wind. Still, she'd called it Pirate Cave and the name had stuck. With a sigh, he scanned the palm trees growing at the edge of the beach then looked out to sea again.

'I mean it, Alfie – what will we do if we find her?' Once more, Fleur tried to be logical. If Pearl was stranded in an inlet, how would she and Alfie figure out a way to reunite her with her pod?

'I'll stay with her, that's what. I won't leave her by herself.'

'And what if …?'

'Don't!' He didn't want to risk hearing her say the word 'shark'. 'Come on – let's go.'

She followed more slowly, picking her way between rock pools and steadying herself by placing her hands on the rocks and easing herself down on to the beach. Halfway down, she glanced into the water and saw the tarpon open its gaping mouth to gulp down an unwary silverside. And then, completely unexpectedly and to her total dismay, she saw something else – a huge shadow gliding out from under an overhang, indistinct among the sea grass – something huge and menacing.

'Alfie, wait!' she cried in a voice strangled by

sudden panic.

The shadow emerged from the wafting grass –
unbelievably long and sinuous, snaking silently along
the seabed with the tarpon in its sights. It came out of
the shadow of the rock – a bluish-green creature with a
broad head and a blunt snout and the telltale stripes
down the sides of its body. The shark was in no hurry.
In fact it moved lazily and ominously towards its prey.

'It's here!' Fleur breathed.

Alfie retraced his steps. He stared down at the
underwater hunt going on before their eyes – a tiger
shark in deliberate pursuit of a big, ugly tarpon. The
shark paddled with its long, thin fins, slowly creeping
forward – so long, strong and huge.

They watched in silence. It was like a slow-motion
video – the shark edging forwards, the tarpon unaware
of the enemy among shoals of shining silversides. Rays
of sunlight penetrated far below the surface, dappling
the shark's back. Then there was a sudden change.
The cloud of silversides sensed danger. They darted
away in every direction, quick flashes of silver light
under the surface, leaving the slow-moving tarpon

marooned above the murky sea grass.

Faster than the eye could follow, the shark sped in for the kill. With a quick flick of its tail, it was on the tarpon. It prodded once with its snout then rapidly opened its jaws, snapping them shut to swallow the fish whole.

Alfie let out a groan. Fleur closed her eyes. When she opened them again, there was nothing on the surface of the water to show what had just happened and no sign that the shark had ever been there. The shoals of tiny silver fish quickly reformed and swam on across the bay.

Now there was a fresh dilemma for Alfie and Fleur. Should they stay on Pirate Cave beach, hoping to keep track of the tiger shark, or should they carry on searching for Pearl?

'Let's stay here for a while in case the shark hangs around,' Fleur suggested. 'Then at least we'd know where it is.'

Alfie disagreed. 'They don't stay in one place for very long. You know that.'

It was true – tiger sharks didn't have a home territory but powered on across entire oceans in their

search for food. 'OK, you win. Let's carry on.'

So they trudged on across Pirate Cave Beach then climbed over more rocks into Black Crab Cove. This was a narrow inlet only about fifty metres wide and surrounded by tall cliffs, with the spectacular rock arch at the far end that Mia had christened earlier that morning.

'It seems ages since we drew the new map,' Fleur said with a sigh. Despite her fears for Pearl, she took time to study the natural archway. It was formed of hard black rock and soared at least ten metres into the air. Wind and rain had created it by slowly nibbling away at the surrounding softer rock to leave the graceful arch that they saw now. Ferns and grasses grew in its crevices and birds were attracted to the insects hidden there – she noticed two black cormorants perched on its highest point and a pair of grey pigeons winging their way underneath. At the foot of the rock stack rising from the sea she spotted a pelican, wings spread wide to sun itself on a narrow ledge. It stared down into the water until a fish came along, when it lurched from the ledge and plunged out of sight.

Meanwhile, Alfie's attention was drawn to a deep channel through the sand made by the waves at high tide. The water had thrown heaps of jetsam up against the cliffs – bits of polystyrene and decaying palm fronds, a coil of rusty wire and a mountain of plastic bottles. The second thing that he noticed as he transferred his attention back to the arch was that there seemed to be a way to climb up it. 'I'm going up there, where the cormorants are,' he told Fleur. 'Are you coming?'

She hesitated. 'Are you sure? It looks pretty dangerous.'

'Yes, but we'll be able to see for miles.' It was the reason that ships' boys used to climb to the crow's nest – to get the best view in every direction.

Fleur pressed her lips together then nodded. *Better go with him*, she thought. *We're both good climbers. And he's right – we'll definitely get a great view.*

With the sun past its peak and slowly starting to sink towards Mystery Mountain, they crossed the sand together. They felt water lap around their ankles as they approached the base of the arch. Waves swelled fifty metres out to sea, rolled and broke against the perpendicular stack of rock, sending up cool spray that showered down on their faces and shoulders.

'That feels good,' Fleur murmured as she prepared to follow Alfie in a steep climb to the top.

He steadied himself and picked his footholds carefully, checking that the clumps of grass growing in the crevices didn't dislodge when he stepped on them. It scared him to hear stones come loose beneath his feet and he had to yell a warning to Fleur to watch out. She dodged them by pressing herself close to the rock and waiting for them to rattle past her, down into the sea. Their bodies were damp with sea spray and sweat as they completed the climb.

'We did it!' Fleur sighed with relief. Her legs were shaky and she had a graze on her right ankle where she'd scraped it against the rock, but the view that greeted her was worth it. 'Wow!' she gasped as she pinned her hair behind her ears then looked down at the foaming water.

From his new perch on Magic Arch, Alfie looked out towards the horizon. *Think how cool it would be if we spotted Pearl and her pod,* he thought. *Imagine her cruising towards us with Stormy and Jazz and she whistles up to let me know she's OK. Or say she swims right under the arch, happy as anything, and turns belly-up then flips over again and does her roll trick. Now that would be magic!*

If wishing could have made Pearl appear, she would be there now, chirping up at them. As it was, the ocean was empty as far as the eye could see. The cormorants circled overhead and gulls cried from the cliffs surrounding the cove but there was nothing under the surface of the clear green water except the usual silversides and flashes of electric blue angelfish.

'Maybe we should climb back down.' Fleur suggested quietly. They'd been there for ages and, though there was a breeze to keep them cool, she knew their skin would burn if they stayed much longer.

Alfie frowned. 'You know what's the worst thing about all this?'

She nodded. 'Yes – it's not knowing.'

'Right. If we only *knew* what had happened to Pearl ...'

'But we don't.' Fleur took a deep breath. In Alfie's techie world, every question had an answer and every problem could be solved. He found comfort in maps and calendar sticks, in chipping away at a log to make a canoe that they could sail away in. 'Sorry, Alfie – we really don't.'

*

Alfie and Fleur arrived back at base camp just as the sun set behind the mountain.

Mia saw their two silhouettes appear on the headland and ran hopefully to meet them. 'Did you find her?' she cried.

Fleur replied with a weary shake of her head. 'No, Pearl's still missing.'

'But we saw the shark,' Alfie mumbled. The fruitless search and the shock of seeing the tiger shark hunt down the unsuspecting tarpon had exhausted him and he hung his head as he made his way to the campfire, where Katie greeted him with a quick hug.

'Sit down,' she told him. 'And, Fleury, put your bag down and have something to eat.' She handed them both slices of jackfruit and some mashed crab meat served on broad, shiny leaves. 'Your dad will be here soon so we have to save some for him.'

Quiet for once, Mia sat between Alfie and Fleur. Firelight flickered on their faces as dusk drew in and an evening mist crept down from Mystery Mountain. By the time James had made his way down from Lookout Point, the wind had changed direction and there was a chill in the air.

'It looks like rain.' He pointed to the bank of dark blue clouds outlined by brilliant orange gathering over the mountain. 'I've built up the lookout fire to burn through till morning. I reckon we'll have to batten down the hatches tonight.'

Fleur sighed. A full-on tropical storm seemed a fitting ending to a miserable day. She was footsore, the graze on her ankle still smarted and, as expected, the back of her neck tingled with what felt like sunburn. And now, to cap it all, the whole family would have to huddle all night inside George's Cave while lightning flashed and thunder roared.

'What do you say we get an early night?' Katie suggested as she put fresh logs on the fire. The flames threw a warm light on the partly built shelter and the unfinished canoe that lay under some overhanging palm trees.

Fleur glanced in the direction of the canoe and spied two macaques hiding behind it with only the tufts on the tops of their heads and their gleaming eyes visible. She saw the whisk of a long tail then a third monkey sprang out of the shadows and squatted cheekily inside the canoe.

'What do you three want, as if I didn't know?' She got up to shoo them away. 'There's no food here for you. You'll have to find your own.'

The three monkeys didn't budge. With their heads cocked to one side, they watched her wave her arms and heard her tell them to scram with a look that said, *What's up? We've got as much right to be here as you have.*

Fleur stopped and thought again. 'So, you win,' she decided, hands on hips. 'Just don't go near our food store, OK?' When she turned around, she saw that the others had already set off for George's Cave. She watched Alfie split off and make his way to the water's edge so she followed him and joined him there.

He stared straight ahead without saying anything.

Fleur too was quiet. She thought for the first time of how bad she would feel if it was Jazz that had gone missing instead of Pearl. Her whole world would change – she wouldn't be able to think about anything except where Jazz was and what had happened to him. Was he lost? Was he sick or injured? Was he still alive? The last thought sent a shiver up and down her spine – the idea that she would never see her beloved Jazz again would break her heart. 'Don't worry – we'll try again tomorrow,' she whispered. 'We won't give up until we find her.'

Alfie blinked but didn't speak. A huge, pale moon hung low in the sky over the flat, empty horizon. The waves broke and crashed against the reef. Suddenly a dolphin leaped high in the air. One, two, three others soared clear of the water, dark grey in the fading light. They were joined by eight or ten more – adults and half-grown calves, surging through the white foam and swimming parallel to the shore, from one side of the bay to the other.

Fleur pointed to the lead dolphin. 'That's Marina.' She soon checked off Stormy and Jazz in the group behind. When Jazz broke away from the group to head towards the shore, another adult swiftly rounded him up and brought him back to the pod.

Alfie watched Jazz rise out of the water to do his special tail-walking trick. Fleur's dolphin danced across the bay in the silver moonlight as if to say, *I might not be allowed to come and say hello, but here I am! Look at me.* Meanwhile, the others followed their leader towards Echo Cave Bay.

'Still no Pearl.' Fleur's quiet voice confirmed what Alfie already knew. 'Maybe tomorrow,' she added.

They stood for a while longer. A strong wind far out to sea began to whip the waves into a frenzy. Great rollers crested in ribbons of white foam then broke spectacularly against the reef. Cold rain began to fall. And there, in amongst the churning, heaving waves, they saw the dreaded shark cut through the water, its fin and broad back clearly visible as it swam terrifyingly close to the shore. Alfie and Fleur made out its razor-sharp tail fluke, the menacing twists and turns of its long, lithe body.

Holding his breath, Alfie followed its slow progress across the bay – solitary king of all it surveyed.

Chapter Nine

For Alfie, nothing on Dolphin Island could be the same without Pearl.

He sat through the storm that night hardly noticing the rain that lashed down from thunderous skies or the wind that whipped up the sand. He didn't flinch as lightning flashed and he watched without reacting as waves dashed sodden palm fronds, coconuts and waterlogged branches up to the mouth of George's Cave.

Fleur and James dragged them clear of the entrance, only to find another wave carried more debris towards them. Then it was Katie and Mia's turn to dash out and salvage wood that could be used later for the fires, getting soaked to the skin as they braved the storm. Meanwhile, Alfie sat in a corner, ignoring everything.

By dawn the storm had lifted. The sky was a gentle

pink. There were no clouds – only mist drifting down from the mountain to meet plumes of white smoke rising from the main campfire. At the foot of the cliff a heavy palm frond had torn free from a nearby tree and dropped on to the new shelter, knocking down a section of wall.

When Mia emerged from the cave and spotted this, she called for Alfie to come. 'Something's happened to the shelter. Alfie, I'm not joking – you have to come and look.'

Reluctantly he came out and inspected the damage. So, *a wall's down – so what?* He shrugged then went to the shoreline to splash his face with water. He didn't even check the bay to see if there were dolphins nearby.

It was Fleur and Mia who tried to fix the wall panel while Katie and James set about the morning's chores – James to carry firewood up to Lookout Point and Katie to catch snappers in her home-made fishing net.

'We'll have to mend this big hole.' Crouching over the panel, Fleur pointed out the damage then reached for some dried palm fronds. Normally Alfie would be here with them, working out how to strengthen the walls so they didn't fall down during the next storm. But today he'd turned his back on them and stood silently at the water's edge, head hanging, ignoring everyone.

'What's wrong with Alfie?' Mia asked as she watched Fleur weave the fronds in and out of the bamboo supports. 'Is he still thinking about Pearl?'

Fleur nodded. 'I said we'd go and look for her again.'

'When?'

'Later on today.'

'Can I come?' Mia jumped in with her quick-fire questions. 'Where shall we look? Will we see the shark?'

'Slow down,' Fleur warned. 'Yes, you can come, but we have to do our jobs first. Why don't you fetch some jackfruit while I finish mending this?'

With a nod and a smile, Mia set off eagerly up the cliff path.

'Say hi to Dad when you reach Lookout Point,' Fleur called after her. 'Let him know where you're going.'

Mia didn't turn.

Perhaps she hadn't heard, but it probably didn't matter – their dad was bound to spot Mia's bright red feathers and turquoise swimmie on her way up. So Fleur worked on until Alfie finally wandered up the beach to join her. He walked towards the canoe and rolled it over with his foot then gave it a kick with the sole of his foot.

'Stupid boat,' he muttered, delivering a second kick. 'It's not going to be any good. Never was, never will be.'

'Don't say that.' To Fleur, Alfie saying this about the canoe was a sign that he'd given up on everything – on being rescued, on getting back home, and especially on ever seeing Pearl again. She knew it was important to talk him round. 'I'll help you with it tonight, after we get back.'

'Get back from where?' He glowered at her from under a thick tangle of hair that had fallen over his forehead.

'From Black Crab Cove or wherever we end up looking for Pearl.'

'What makes you think we'll find her today if we didn't yesterday?'

Fleur ignored the question. 'We can go further than Black Crab Cove this time. We'll find a way under Magic Arch into the next bay and the bay after that until we reach Land's End. We'll look in every single place we can think of.'

He stared angrily at her as if it was her fault that Pearl had disappeared. 'Marina and the others were swimming north last night. Why should we head south again?'

'I don't know, Alfie.' Fleur gave an exasperated sigh. 'I just think it's worth carrying on south. Then, if we don't find her, we could head north tomorrow.'

He thrust his hair back from his forehead, making it stick up on end. 'OK,' he said sullenly. Then he narrowed his eyes and checked himself. 'Sorry – I'm worried about her, that's all.'

'I know. I would be too if Jazz went missing. But we're not going to give up.'

He nodded slowly then rolled the canoe the right way up. 'Sorry,' he said again.

'We *will* find out what's happened to Pearl.' Fleur looked steadily into his eyes, which had softened and gazed pleadingly back at her.

He responded with the phrase and gesture that they'd used to swear promises when they were small. 'Hand on heart?'

'Hand on heart,' she echoed. She put her hand to her chest and felt the strong, even beat of her heart. 'So help me mend this wall. The sooner we finish our jobs here, the sooner we can set off and look.'

*

'Mia ought to be back by now.' Fleur judged the time by the position of the sun in the sky.

'Why – where did she go?' Alfie had fixed the wall panel back in position and was now eager to resume the search for Pearl. He checked that they had full water bottles and slices of coconut to take with them.

'She went to find jackfruit.' Guessing that it had been more than an hour since Mia had left, Fleur began to wonder what had kept her. 'We can't set off until she gets back.'

'Why not?' He jammed his knife into the waistband of his shorts then tied his dad's red and white spotted kerchief around his head.

'Because I said she could come with us.'

Alfie frowned. 'She'll slow us down,' he grumbled.

'Even so.' A promise was a promise. 'Listen; you wait here while I run and fetch her.'

But hanging around at base camp was the last thing that Alfie wanted to do. 'Why don't I set off?' he suggested. 'I'll only go as far as Black Crab Cove, then, if you and Mia haven't caught up with me, I'll wait by Magic Arch.'

'OK.' She didn't like it, but she understood why Alfie was impatient. 'But, definitely wait there.'

They agreed then went off in different directions – Alfie towards the Turtle Beach headland and Fleur up the cliff path. She climbed quickly, only pausing for a refreshing drink by Butterfly Falls before heading on towards Lookout Point. She guessed that Mia had forgotten all about their planned expedition and that she would find her there with their dad. Mia was like that – happily scatterbrained, easily changing her plans if something more exciting came along.

When Fleur reached the high ledge, the lookout fire burned strongly and there was a big stack of firewood nearby. But there was no sign of either her dad or her sister. She sighed then turned to scan Turtle Beach. There was Alfie, on a mission, jogging on towards Pirate Cave Beach, his red shorts and bandana easily visible. She turned again to search the empty expanse of burned scrubland leading up to the forest. *Maybe Dad went with Mia to find the fruit and they forgot about the time.* Cupping her hands around her mouth, she yelled their names. 'Mia, Dad – where are you?'

There was no answer and nothing for it except to set off after them. So Fleur picked her way up the ash-covered slope, heading for the place where the jackfruit trees grew. The breeze lifted ash from the ground and blew it straight into her face. Soon she had dust up her nostrils and in her mouth – a gritty residue that she spat out. But she was close to the fruit trees now so she called a second time. 'Whoo-hoo, Mia, Dad – it's me!'

Still no answer, but her yell disturbed a small flock of cockatoos hidden behind the broad leaves of the jackfruit trees. They squawked as they flapped down the hillside towards her, quickly followed by snorts and snuffles from the bushes underneath. Though at first she didn't see them, Fleur recognized the sounds of wild boar foraging through the undergrowth – nothing else made that kind of noise or barged clumsily through the bushes. And sure enough, after she'd waited for a minute or so, a small boar came into view – a barrel-shaped creature with light brown fur, short legs and dainty trotters. Tempted by the rotting jackfruit lying under the nearest tree, the young boar ignored her and was soon followed by three others, two adults and an even smaller baby, who came trotting out of the bushes with an excited squeal. The adults lifted their heads to scent the air then spotted Fleur. Deciding she was harmless, they chose to ignore her and were soon gobbling down the tasty fruit with satisfied grunts.

Fleur was relieved to see that life in the forest had returned to normal after the fire. But it scared her too. 'Normal' life meant monkeys and possums, tree kangaroos and bowerbirds, butterflies and bats. But it also meant that the dreaded mystery creature might have returned, so her heart skipped a beat as she gritted her teeth and walked reluctantly on.

As she reached the edge of the forest, she decided the best thing to do was to make lots of noise. 'Dad, Mia, where are you?' Remembering the time when Mia had played a trick on her, Fleur picked up a stout stick and swished at the nearest bushes, making the family of wild boars skitter back into the undergrowth. More parrots rose from the tree canopy and flew away.

Fleur hesitated. She felt the sun on her back as she breathed in the damp coolness of the shadowy forest ahead. Suppose Mia wasn't in there after all? Perhaps she'd forgotten about the jackfruit and gone off with their dad in another direction. Listening intently, Fleur heard nothing to suggest that she was on the right track. *Deep breaths*, she thought. *Think this through. Is it worth going any further, or shall I just give up and go back to the beach?*

But no, she couldn't do that. What if Mia hadn't spoken to their dad at all but had entered the jungle alone and got lost? Maybe she'd been gathering jackfruit, seen the small boar family foraging at the edge of the forest and followed them in. It was easy to lose your way once you entered – the leaves overhead cast deep shadows and the tree roots were thick and twisted. Low-hanging creepers got in your way and tripped you up. Mia might have fallen and hurt herself …

Fleur ducked under a low branch and ventured forward, using her stick to push aside a prickly bush and her free hand to brush a stinging insect from her leg. The air felt damp. It was laden with heavy, cloying scents from scarlet and pink flowers that blossomed in the patch of oozing mud ahead. *Oh, Mi-mi*, she thought, *please tell me I'm wrong ...*

A loud scream broke through the buzz of insects. A long, loud, high-pitched scream.

'Mia!' Fleur forged ahead. She stepped into the mud and sank almost knee-deep, lifted one foot and managed to ease it up on to a log before dragging herself clear.

There was another scream – more of a wail this time – and the sound of someone rushing through the bushes. Fleur saw a flash of turquoise then a clear view of Mia's terrified face, mouth open, eyes wide as she gasped for breath. Fleur lunged towards her and caught her around the waist.

'Monster!' Mia gasped. She trembled and hid her face against Fleur's chest. 'Here in the jungle. Monster!'

Without thinking, Fleur gripped her wrist and stumbled back through the swamp. Thick mud sucked at their feet and tried to pull them down. Gasping for breath and with their hearts racing, they ducked low and stumbled back into the sunlight.

*

'What kind of monster?' Fleur asked once she was able to draw breath. Her mouth was dry and her heart thumped against her ribs.

Out in the open, Mia still clung to Fleur's hand. 'Big!' she stammered. 'With giant teeth. It tried to bite me.'

'Calm down.' Fleur looked with dread towards the forest but there was no sign of the monster following them. 'How big – this big?' She spread her arms out wide and waited for Mia's reply.

'Bigger.' Mia shuddered at the memory.

'What colour was it?'

'Browny-green. I don't really know. It was hiding behind a tree so I couldn't see all of it.' She squeezed her eyes tight shut.

'It's all right, I won't ask you any more questions.' Fleur patted her hand, then, with a final glance back at the forest, began to lead her down the slope. 'Why didn't you stop and tell Dad where you were going, like I told you?'

'I didn't hear you.' Scared that she would get into trouble, Mia began to cry.

'And he didn't spot you on the cliff path.' Fleur realized what had happened. 'So you went up the mountain by yourself, looking for fruit. What happened then?'

'I saw a baby pig. He was cute so I followed him.'

'OK. But you shouldn't have gone into the jungle without one of us.' Relief seeped in through Fleur's fear and dread. Mia was safe – that was what mattered.

'Is that a rule?'

'It is – it's my most important rule. Mum and Dad's most important rule is no swimming. Mine is no going into the forest alone.' Looking down at Mia's tear-stained face, Fleur relented. 'Don't worry – no one's going to tell you off. Everyone will be glad that nothing bad happened to you.'

Mia let out a loud sigh then suddenly stopped and tugged at Fleur's hand. 'We forgot the jackfruit.'

'Never mind that now. We have to go and help Alfie look for Pearl.'

As if by magic, Mia's expression changed. Her smile

came back as she broke free then charged ahead. 'Yay!' she cried. She ran ahead, kicking up ash as she went.

Fleur took a last glance over her shoulder. There really was a jungle monster living up there – Mia had just given her the proof. And there was also a monster of the deep – a tiger shark – in the shallow water close to the shore. A land monster and a sea monster. Fleur took a deep breath and hurried on.

*

It was late in the afternoon when Fleur and Mia joined Alfie in Black Crab Cove. He lay on his stomach on top of Magic Arch, gazing down into the deep water beneath.

'Any luck?' Fleur called across the small beach.

'*Luck-luck-luck.*' Her voice echoed around the cove, against the high rocks and back again.

'Not yet.' He stayed on his precarious perch until Mia and Fleur reached the arch. He'd waited there for what felt like hours, studying every square metre, from the foaming water around the rock stack beneath him right out to the horizon. He'd followed the progress of a tiny container ship from north to south – much too far away for him to signal to it for help. With a sinking heart he'd watch it turn into a pale speck then disappear.

'Come down and talk to us,' Fleur told him. 'Then we can decide what to do next.'

So he climbed down to the beach and stood with the others in the shadow of the rocks. 'What kept you?' he grumbled.

'I saw a monster in the jungle!' Mia was eager to deliver a blow-by-blow account. 'It was hu-u-uge! It hissed at me. It's got big teeth and long claws.'

Alfie glanced uneasily at Fleur.

'She did,' Fleur confirmed. 'I didn't see it but I believe her.'

'That's all we need,' he said with a scowl. 'It means we can't fetch firewood from the forest any more.'

'Or lianas, or anything else,' Fleur pointed out. 'From now on we'll have to rely on what we find on the beaches.'

He nodded. 'There's plenty of driftwood on the next beach. I could see it from the top of the arch.'

'But it's too far away from base camp for us to carry it back,' Fleur pointed out. 'We'd never make it before the sun goes down.'

'OK, but I want to keep on looking for Pearl,' Alfie insisted. From the top of the arch he'd studied the neighbouring bay and picked out a strip of wet sand bordered by mangroves – strange, low trees with overhanging branches and twisted roots rising out of swampy, brown water.

'Anyway, there's no way on to that beach, is there?' Fleur looked up at the rock face rising sheer out of the sand and saw that it was impossible to climb.

'Yes, there is – there's a ledge under the arch.' Alfie had had plenty of time to work it out. 'I reckon we could do it that way.'

Fleur and Mia made out a narrow ledge just clear of the water. Swirling eddies to the left and overhanging rock to the right would make it tricky but they could probably manage it.

'OK, we've just got time,' Fleur agreed. She let Alfie go on ahead and put Mia in the middle, warning her to be careful. 'Watch where Alfie puts his feet and don't lean out too far over the water. Take it easy – don't rush.'

A fearless Mia followed close in her big brother's footsteps, ignoring heavy spray from waves breaking close by and jumping down into Alfie's arms when she reached the end of the ledge.

Stepping down into Mangrove Bay was like entering a different world. Instead of tall, straight palm trees fringing pure white sand there was a network of bent and twisted trunks growing out of dark brown water. Their leaves were broad and flat and their massive roots snaked into the air, creating a mesh of dark arches for whatever creatures lived beneath them.

'What are they?' Mia murmured as Alfie waded across a deep channel of murky water that ran swiftly from the trees towards the sea. He was up to his waist and in danger of being swept off his feet.

'They're mangrove trees,' Fleur told her. 'Here, hold my hand.' Together they safely crossed the saltwater stream then followed Alfie up to the edge of the swamp.

Their arrival set off a noisy, squawking chorus from parakeets nesting in the branches. Frogs croaked unseen in amongst the tangled roots and a colony of small black and white monkeys sprang out at them,

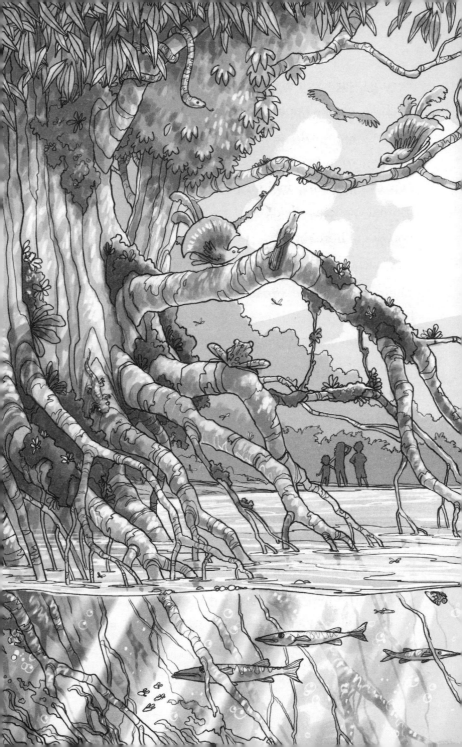

baring their teeth and chattering angrily.

'Hey, cool – capuchins!' Fleur greeted the sight of the monkeys with a surprised grin. Their pink faces were surrounded by fluffy white hair and topped by a cap of black fur, making them the cutest of all the monkey species she'd seen in wildlife videos. 'What are you doing here?'

The largest monkey stopped dead. He clutched a long sugarcane which he held up in front of him as if brandishing a sword.

'We don't want a fight,' Fleur said with a laugh as the rest of the group gathered behind their leader. She noticed crab shells scattered over the sand – the remains of a recent capuchin meal.

The leader swiped at Mia with the cane. *Swish!*

Mia ducked then rolled out of reach.

Fleur pulled her on to her feet. 'You don't belong here, Mr Capuchin,' she insisted. This type of monkey usually lived thousands of miles away in places like Costa Rica and Argentina. 'What happened? Did you get shipwrecked, just like us?'

The male monkey tilted his head to one side and

stared at her. Behind him, a baby ventured down from its mother's back then crept to the front for a better view of the intruders, but when two more youngsters broke ranks, their mothers pulled them back into line.

'We won't stick around for long,' Fleur promised, sensing that Alfie was getting impatient. 'We're planning to check out the mangroves to make sure that Pearl hasn't got stranded in there.'

'You two wait here – I'll do it,' Alfie said with an exasperated sigh. He bent low under the branches and waded into the swamp.

Fleur and Mia heard cane toads croak and saw them plop into the water in every direction. Tree squirrels leaped nimbly from branch to branch. The mangrove swamp was alive with wildlife – but was the water deep enough for a dolphin to survive?

Alfie looked up at a dense canopy of leaves. The water reached his waist and then his chest before he met a solid obstacle in the shape of a boulder submerged below the surface. Trying to make his way around it, he decided that he'd reached a dead end and turned back.

He emerged on to the beach to see that the capuchins had lost interest in Mia and Fleur. The whole colony had moved on to the headland and was following the alpha male up Magic Arch without a backwards glance.

Fleur tore herself away from the monkey spectacle. 'Well?'

'Nothing,' he reported. 'I only found one channel deep enough for Pearl to swim up and she wasn't there.'

Though Fleur wasn't surprised, she didn't say so. She realized that for Alfie's sake they had to follow every possible lead. 'Sorry,' she murmured.

He sighed and shook his head. 'I won't give up,' he warned as he jutted out his chin and stared out to sea.

'Neither will we,' Fleur promised. The shadows cast by the mangroves were creeping further down the beach – at this rate they would have to hurry to reach home before sunset. 'We'll try again tomorrow, then the day after and the day after that.'

'I'll *never* give up,' Alfie vowed as he waded across the fast-flowing stream. 'I won't let her down!'

Chapter Ten

'Whoever said life on Dolphin Island was easy?' During breakfast next day James cut short the kids' everyday moans and groans. 'Mi-mi, I know you don't want to collect wood for the fires, but it has to be done.'

'Why can't I do it later?' Mia protested.

'Because the fires will go out if you don't go now. Then what?' He dished out scrambled eggs and dried fish, pretending to bop her on the head with his spoon. 'Cheer up. You can all go and look for Pearl as soon as you've done your jobs.'

Fleur let the conversation float over her head. She was glad of the early morning mist that drifted in from the sea – at least it would stay cool while she collected water and gathered coconuts from under the trees at the edge of Base Camp Bay.

'The trick is to stay cheerful even when things don't go your way,' their dad advised. 'There's an old song about that – "Smile though your heart is aching ..."' He put the spoon against his lips, pretending it was a microphone, then crooned the words in a deep, slow voice.

Mia clamped her hands over her ears. 'Da-ad!' She jumped up and ran to catch up with Alfie who had already finished breakfast and was scaling the headland into Turtle Bay.

James covered one side of his face with his hand, grimaced at Fleur then winked. 'Oops, was it something I said?'

Their dad enjoyed embarrassing them whenever he got the chance so Fleur grinned at him as she picked up two big containers then set off up the cliff path. What day was today, she wondered. She was losing track. Was it Day 48 or 49? Counting back to Mia's birthday, she reckoned it must be 49 – a Sunday. Hmm, it didn't really matter anyway. Here the days merged into one another. *Wake up, splash face with seawater, eat breakfast, begin chores. Build shelter.*

Sleep. Wake up … Fleur sighed as she glanced down through the mist to see that the recently mended wall was still in place. *Build shelter*, she repeated to herself. That meant that it would probably be past midday before they were allowed to set off in search of Pearl again. 'Poor Pearl, poor Alfie,' she murmured as she climbed on up the steep path.

Down on Turtle Beach, Alfie and Mia found plenty of driftwood among the usual heaps of plastic bottles. They picked up planks and tree branches worn smooth by the waves before being dumped on the shore.

'Ouch!' As she dragged a branch towards the headland, Mia stubbed her toe on a rock hidden by the mist.

Alfie found her hopping on one leg and holding her injured toe. 'Here – let me take a look.'

'Ouch, ouch!' she cried as she offered him her foot. 'Is it bleeding?'

He nodded. 'A bit.' In fact, there was a deep graze that would have to be kept clean. So he took off his red bandana and made a clumsy bandage to cover the wound. 'Hop up on my back. I'll give you a piggyback.'

'It stings!' she wailed as she hoisted herself up.

With her arms tight around his neck, he carried her over the headland. 'You're heavier than you look,' he complained as he staggered on to Base Camp Bay then on towards the campfire where their dad took over.

'Uh-oh – wounded soldier.' Straight away James saw the problem and sat Mia down on the edge of the platform. He took one of the containers that Fleur had just brought back from Butterfly Falls, poured a little of the water into a coconut shell then untied the bandana and dipped it in. 'This might sting a bit more but then it'll start to feel better,' he promised as he dabbed at the wound.

'What do you want us to do now, Dad?' Fleur asked.

Alfie jumped in with the answer. 'Let's go back for the wood that Mia and I collected.' He set off at a run with Fleur close behind. But when he reached the pile he found that the rising tide had surrounded it and sent many of the planks and branches floating out to sea. He was about to wade in to fetch them when Fleur pulled him back.

'We can't go in the water, remember.'

'I won't go far.' He reached out and caught hold of the nearest branch.

'Not even that far.' Though the mist was clearing, it still hung low over the headland. 'We don't know if the shark's out there. Alfie, you'd better come back.'

He gave a disgusted grunt but he returned to the shore then flung the branch down on to the beach. 'How come nothing's going right today?'

'Yeah, I know what you mean.' Even the weather and the tide seemed to be against them. Fleur watched to see if the waves would wash more of their firewood back on to the beach. Then something made her lift her gaze and stare out to sea – she didn't know what it was, just a sixth sense, a strong feeling that an important event was about to happen.

'What are you looking at?' Alfie asked impatiently.

Instead of answering, Fleur watched the mist swirl higher then slowly burn off in the heat of the sun until the reef off Base Camp Bay gradually materialized. She made out the crescent of dark rocks surrounded by mighty breaking waves and then the watery horizon beyond. The strange, intuitive feeling grew stronger.

Alfie studied her face. She seemed to be holding her breath and waiting. Her brown eyes were wide open and she bit her bottom lip, letting the strengthening breeze blow strands of hair across her cheeks without brushing them back.

'Look!' she whispered.

Two dolphins swam out from behind the reef, heading straight towards them. They disappeared into a lingering patch of low mist then re-emerged, swimming at top speed and calling shrilly to attract Alfie and Fleur's attention – an uninterrupted high whistle from Stormy and a high-low, two-tone call from her very own Jazz.

Fleur felt an instant surge of delight run through her. Forgetting all about their mum and dad's instructions, she dashed into the sea with her arms stretched wide.

Five metres from the shore, Jazz came to a stop. He greeted her with excited clicks, creaks and whistles, then with quick flicks of his tail he circled around her.

Fleur reached out her hand and stroked the velvety

dome of his head. 'I've missed you,' she whispered.

Alfie watched enviously from the shore as Fleur and Jazz said their hellos. He saw that Stormy, who was usually so pushy, had hung back and was swimming back and forth across the bay, as if keeping watch.

'So much!' Fleur said with a sigh. She'd missed the soft feel of Jazz's skin, his downturned mouth and dark, intelligent eyes. Most of all, she'd missed swimming with him in the crystal-clear water.

Jazz nudged her with his beak. He let her pat and cuddle him then broke away and swam further from the shore, tempting her to follow.

'No, you're not allowed,' Alfie reminded her. He kept his eyes on Stormy, who had set up an odd yelp as he slapped his tail flukes against the surface of the water.

'Hey, Jazz – I can't come and play!' Fleur said sadly. 'I bet you shouldn't be here either, not while the shark's around.'

He swam back to her, clicking and pleading.

'I can't,' she told him again before she allowed a new glimmer of hope to enter her head. 'Unless this visit means that the danger's passed. What do you think, Alfie? Do these two know something we don't?'

He shook his head. There was something odd about the noise Stormy was making. It was more of a warning call than a friendly greeting. And he was still patrolling the bay, keeping a careful watch. 'No,' he decided. 'That's not what they're trying to tell us. I think it's the opposite.'

'What – that the shark's still hanging around?' She cast a quick, anxious glance at Jazz and Stormy then looked out to the reef.

'I don't know for sure, but it could be.' Alfie too felt his stomach tie itself in knots as he searched the horizon.

Fleur held her breath and scanned the waves. As far as she could tell, there was no sharp tail fin cutting through the water or any other evidence of the tiger shark cruising around the rocks. 'All clear,' she breathed.

'Are you sure?' High tide meant that the reef was taking a pounding from the waves. 'Sometimes it's hard to tell the difference between a rock and a shark's fin in amongst all that foam.'

Resting her hand on Jazz's broad back, she searched again. 'I can't see anything sinister.'

'So why is Stormy acting weird?' he asked.

Mia's dolphin surged towards them then turned and sped back towards the headland separating them from Pirate Cave Beach. He did it twice more to ensure that Alfie and Fleur understood what he wanted them to do.

'I get it. We have to go with you,' Alfie said as Stormy approached them one more time.

The dark grey dolphin clapped his jaws together and waited for Alfie to climb on to his back.

Alfie frowned then looked at Fleur. 'Does this mean that they know where Pearl is?'

'Probably.' She nodded slowly.

'We have to let them take us there, whatever Mum and Dad say.'

'I know.'

'We have to go now!'

'I know, Alfie!' Fleur tried to block out the risks but only succeeded in conjuring up a close-up image of the vicious shark surging towards her, its jaws yawning open to reveal its killer teeth.

'Now!' he repeated as, without a second thought, he made a lunge towards Stormy and clambered on to his back. They set off for the headland ahead of Fleur and Jazz.

Taking a deep breath, Fleur hauled herself on to Jazz's back then felt him set off with a sudden burst of speed. Blinded by cold spray, she kept her head down and held tight to his fin until they drew level with the others. Together they swam around the rocks into the neighbouring bay.

'OK, where now?' A quick glance down into the clear depths told Alfie that they were surrounded by a shoal of parrotfish. Waves broke heavily on to the sandy beach.

Once more Stormy took the lead. He forged ahead with Alfie and followed the coastline until they reached Black Crab Cove.

Alfie glanced over his shoulder at Fleur and Jazz. They were close enough for him to yell over the crashing waves. 'Are you OK?'

'I'm fine.'

'Magic Arch is up ahead. I reckon that's where we're heading.'

'Yes, but why? We've looked there already.'

Jazz swam alongside Stormy towards the arch. They were halfway across the narrow cove when Alfie's grasp on Stormy's fin suddenly tightened. He swallowed hard and took a second look through the arch. *No – please, no!* There, framed by the rock, was the sight they'd dreaded all along. The tiger shark cruised towards them through the brownish waters of Mangrove Bay.

In the same split second Fleur saw it too. Her throat constricted and she couldn't speak. Surely the shark had spotted them. It had probably picked up their approach long ago by minute vibrations in the water as Jazz and Stormy crossed Pirate Cave Beach. It had lain in wait until it had them in its sights.

'Quick, quick – turn around!' Alfie pleaded with Stormy.

The tiger shark held a steady course straight through the arch, where they lost sight of it in amongst breaking waves and white spray.

'Stormy, turn around!'

Jazz and Stormy took no notice. They circled slowly and waited as the shark reappeared and swam so close that Alfie and Fleur could see each tooth in the gaping jaw. They clung to their dolphins, stiff with fear. Then, at the very last moment before the shark could strike, Stormy and Jazz took off. They sprinted away from the enemy, curving out to sea and swimming wide of the stack of rock that supported the arch. The shark gave chase but Fleur and Alfie lost it again in the spray surrounding the rock. All they could do was to cling on and pray.

The dolphins carried them clear of the arch then curved back towards the shoreline. The mangroves were now in sight and the deep, fast-running channel cutting through the wet sand. But now the blunt head of the shark surfaced again, further out to sea. Maybe it was waiting to see what Jazz and Stormy would do next.

Stormy was the first to reach the shore. To Alfie's amazement, he didn't stop there but swam on up the channel, helped by the incoming tide. Soon they entered the stand of mangroves, leaving Jazz and Fleur behind.

'Come on, Jazz, what are you waiting for?' Fleur cried, pressing her legs against his sides. 'Go ahead – follow them!'

But he refused. Instead he watched and waited, making it plain that Alfie and Stormy's job was to explore the mangrove swamp while they guarded the entrance.

Fleur's heart was in her mouth. The shark was waiting and watching offshore and now she and Jazz must face it alone.

Stormy swam on between twisted roots, taking a different route to the one Alfie had chosen the day before. Alfie had to lie flat on his back to avoid the tunnel of low branches until they came to a place where the channel divided and Stormy chose the wider course that opened up on to a small lagoon. Here Alfie could raise his head and take in his surroundings, while back in the bay Jazz and Fleur took up a sentry position across the entrance to the saltwater stream.

Fifty metres out to sea, the shark kept its distance.

Waves broke over its head and crashed against the rocks but it stayed where it was, biding its time.

Inland, the quiet lagoon was surrounded by mangroves and teeming with life. At the far side white egrets stood on one leg in shallow water while all around, tree frogs sat motionless on mangrove roots. Under a clear blue sky Stormy carried Alfie slowly across the warm lagoon until he reached the egrets. Waves lapped against the mesh of thick roots. Stormy came to a halt, then, without warning, he rolled on to his side and tipped his passenger from his back.

Alfie landed with a loud splash in the murky water. When he stood up it came up to his chest. There was slimy mud under his feet and a canopy of broad leaves overhead.

Alfie's heart pounded. He was sure that Pearl must be close by. 'Pearl, it's me.'

He heard a disturbance – the rustle of leaves and the lapping of waves against the mangrove roots. And then there was a quiet, persistent chirping from under an overhanging branch – Pearl's unmistakable whistle. Holding his breath, Alfie moved the branch aside and saw her resting in the shade.

At first it seemed as if nothing was wrong – her eyes were bright and she sounded pleased to see him. But then he looked more closely and saw an ugly gash in her side. There was an open wound running down her flank from her front flipper to her dorsal fin. Savage teeth marks showed where the shark had bitten her.

'Pearl!' He breathed out as he crouched beside her. 'Don't worry – I'm here now.'

He didn't notice Stormy turn around and swim quietly across the lagoon, leaving him alone with Pearl. 'I'll look after you,' he murmured. 'I'll stay here and I won't let anything hurt you, ever.'

Chapter Eleven

For Fleur time seemed to stand still. She'd watched with bated breath as Stormy had carried Alfie out of sight, and then waited with Jazz at the shoreline. Behind them, the powerful shark swam lazily under Magic Arch then around the rock stack and back again, as if it wanted to show them it had plenty of time before it moved in for the kill.

Astride Jazz's back, Fleur watched its progress with a chest that was tight with fear. She turned towards the mangroves. 'Come back, Alfie!' she murmured. 'Let me know what's happening.'

She grew afraid that Stormy and Alfie had got lost in the swamp. *Is it down to me and Jazz?* she wondered. *From now on is it just us against the shark?*

Jazz didn't move. He clicked quietly. Was this him

sending a message to Stormy? Was Mia's dolphin close enough to use echolocation to pick up Jazz's signal? *What in the world is happening?* Fleur's knuckles went white as she clung tightly to Jazz's fin.

Every second felt like a minute. Every minute stretched to an hour.

Then Stormy swam out from under the mangrove trees without Alfie.

Fleur's eyes widened and her heart knocked against her ribs. Scary thoughts flashed through her mind: of Alfie being hit on the head and falling unconscious from Stormy's back or of Alfie tangled up in tree roots and being sucked into the swamp. With a sharp intake of breath she watched Stormy draw near.

He swam down the channel until he reached them. He held his head clear of the water and thrashed his tail against the surface as he whistled a shrill greeting.

'Where's Alfie?' Fleur gasped.

Still calling loudly, Stormy turned and swam back up the narrow channel. Then he turned and rejoined Fleur and Jazz.

'OK, we get it – you've checked that it's safe in

there and Alfie has sent you to let us know. But the question is – do you want us to follow you back in?' Fleur's heart stormed inside her chest as if trying to break through her ribs. Her fingers tingled and her grip lost its strength.

Jazz held his position on the shoreline, aware of the shark cruising slowly towards them. Stormy's whistle rose still higher. Jazz answered by smacking his jaws together – *clap-clap-clap!*

'Let's go and find Alfie. Come on, Jazz – this is urgent!'

Instead of following her command, he reared high out of the water, so fast and sudden that Fleur lost her grip and slithered from his back. She sank below the waves and when she rose to the surface, she saw the two youngsters doing the craziest thing … they were up out of the water, their sleek grey bodies erect, flapping their flippers as they tail-walked side by side towards the shark. The surprise challenge caught it off guard and it let them advance.

Treading water close to the entrance to the bay, Fleur groaned. She couldn't bear to look. She closed

her eyes, counted to five then dared to open them. The shark and the two dolphins were nowhere to be seen. Thinking the worst, she stared out to sea. Eventually she made out Stormy's dark grey, torpedo-shaped body speeding south past Magic Arch towards Land's End. Meanwhile, Jazz headed north towards Black Crab Cove. Their daring trick seemed to have confused the enemy and gained them a bit of time. But where was the tiger shark? Before Fleur could discover the answer, she spotted other dolphins swimming towards Mangrove Bay. They seemed full of purpose, sticking close together and surging through the blue water until they reached the waves that broke against Magic Arch. Fleur recognized Marina at the head of the pod – her large bright eyes and short nostrum, her loud insistent whistle. She swam right up to Fleur and nudged her in the direction of the deep channel that cut across the beach.

Now I get it – I really do! At last Fleur realized that Stormy, Jazz and the rest of the dolphins wanted her to enter the swamp as well. But, as she staggered backwards towards the shore, the shark darted out from under the arch and made a mighty lunge towards Marina. Shock ran through Fleur's body but Pearl's agile mother soared into the air, out of reach of the shark's jaws. She landed back in the water and was instantly surrounded by the pod. A second later they had all dived out of sight.

Now, with her heart in her mouth over the fate of their dolphin friends, Fleur had to leave them to deal with the shark. She made her way up the channel, helped by the incoming tide which carried her swiftly into the shade of the mangrove trees and swept her to a point where the channel split into two. Here she had to make a choice so she caught hold of a gnarled root to steady herself then cupped her hand to her mouth. 'Alfie!' she cried.

The low canopy of branches deadened her voice. There was no reply. But the smaller of the two channels seemed too narrow and shallow for Stormy to have chosen. The wider channel was the one she should take. On she went through the shadows, grabbing hold of roots and propelling herself forward until there was sunlight ahead and the waterway opened out on to a small lagoon.

She looked across a wide, calm stretch of glistening water. 'Alfie!' she yelled.

'Over here!' His voice was faint but unmistakable. 'Head across the lagoon to the far bank. I'm here with Pearl!'

So, with hope rising strongly within her, Fleur struck out in a fast front crawl. She was aware of the fierce sun high in the sky and of tendrils of sea grass pulling at her legs and arms but was determined that nothing would stop her from reaching her brother and his beloved dolphin.

'Over here!' he said again.

Pausing to take a deep gasp of humid air into her lungs, she followed the direction of his voice. Then she got her first sight of them – Alfie up to his chest in water, with one arm slung over a mangrove root and the other hand resting on Pearl's head.

'The shark bit her,' Alfie gabbled as Fleur held her head clear of the water and took another deep breath. 'She's injured.'

Fleur's heart sank again. 'How bad is it?' she asked

as he moved aside to give her a clear view of Pearl wallowing in shallow water at the edge of the lagoon. 'Oh!' She breathed out with a low, groaning sound when she saw the deep wound in Pearl's flank.

'What do we do? How do we help her?' Alfie asked.

'OK, OK – wait!' She gritted her teeth and tried to remember every scrap of dolphin information she'd learned. 'For a start, it might not be as serious as it looks.'

'What are you talking about? How can it not be serious?' He'd had more time to inspect the savage bite – the torn flesh and the deep bite marks – and he *knew* how bad it was. Anyway, why else would Stormy and Jazz have risked their own lives to come and ask for help?

'Because!' she began then faltered. The gash did look deep and ugly. 'Because we're here for a start. We can make sure the shark doesn't swim up into the lagoon while Pearl is here.'

'How – by waving a Harry Potter wand?' To him what Fleur was suggesting seemed impossible.

'I don't know yet. We'll find a way. Second, I can tell

you for a fact that dolphins heal better than humans. Their wounds don't get infected. Marine experts think they've got a natural antibiotic in their bodies. They're not sure how it works but it does. And dolphins have been known to swim and keep afloat with worse bites than this.'

'OK, cool.' He desperately wanted to believe her. 'How do you know all this?'

'I've seen pictures and videos.' Fleur swam close enough to Pearl to stroke her back.

Pearl turned her head towards her and pushed gently with her beak.

'I'm not leaving until she does!' Alfie spoke before Fleur had a chance to say anything else. 'She's saved me before now – in the shipwreck, when I was lost at sea, lots of times – now it's my turn to save her. It's only fair.'

Fleur nodded. 'You're right and we'll do it together.'

Her words brought a lump to his throat. 'Thanks,' he murmured.

'Don't thank me. Thank Stormy and Jazz.' Fleur knew that it was time for them to be practical and think of solutions. 'We have to make this lagoon into a sort of hospital pool to give her time to get better. It has to be a place where the shark can't come.' Looking around, she saw that there was only one entrance. 'It's a good job the mangroves grow so close together. They make a natural barrier. Now we have to block that opening with rocks and branches – to build a kind of wall to keep the shark out.'

Alfie seized on the plan. 'That'll work,' he agreed. 'Shall we take it in turns – one of us stays with Pearl while the other starts building.'

'No. It'll be quicker if we both do it. Pearl will be OK here.'

So Alfie stroked Pearl again and laid his head against hers. 'We won't go far,' he promised. 'You'll still be able to see us.'

Pearl clicked a quiet, calm reply. Seeing Fleur swim out into the middle of the lagoon, she nudged him to encourage him to follow.

Soon both Alfie and Fleur had reached the entrance channel where they hauled themselves out of the murky water and began to search for loose branches and floating logs. They found plenty of driftwood amongst the tangled roots – planks that they could stand upright. So they thrust the first one deep into the sand and jammed it in place by using a heavy stone as a hammer. Soon they had built a rough stockade and could start reinforcing it by threading palm fronds and mangrove branches between the stakes.

'It has to be strong,' Alfie insisted, one eye on Pearl as he and Fleur worked on through the heat of the afternoon. The ebbing tide created a strong undertow that sucked at the base of the barrier. 'We need more rocks.'

Fleur gritted her teeth and carried on building. She tried not to dwell on the hunt that was happening out to sea – the tiger shark in pursuit of Pearl's pod, with her own beautiful Jazz and Mia's Stormy as its prey. As she worked, she made a silent promise to look out for the dolphins, either later that evening or early next morning, to try to let Pearl's pod know that Pearl was safe. But for now it would have to wait.

She and Alfie built the wall higher and stronger until the setting sun began to tinge the fluffy clouds in the west a delicate shade of pink.

'Someone needs to tell Mum and Dad what's happening before it gets dark.' Astride a mangrove root and hammering yet another stake into place, Fleur paused.

'Not me.' No way would Alfie leave Pearl. He glanced across the lagoon and saw her watching him. 'She trusts me to stay with her.'

'OK, I'll go.' Fleur knew she would have to hurry. 'I'll explain about Pearl. But I won't have time to get back here again before dark. I'll have to spend the night in base camp and bring food and water first thing tomorrow morning.'

'Cool,' he muttered, inspecting the barrier for weak spots.

'You'll be OK by yourself?' she checked.

'Yeah, just go.' The wall was as strong as they could make it – it was time for him to get back to Pearl.

So Fleur set off for home. The channel was shallower now that the tide was out and she quickly emerged on to the beach. She hurried across Mangrove Bay then edged under the arch towards the neighbouring beach.

Pausing on the ledge for a moment, she gazed out to sea. A blood-red sun hovered over the shimmering horizon. There was no sign of Marina and her pod or of the dreaded shark. Taking a deep breath, Fleur hurriedly picked her way across the rocks then jumped down on to Pirate Cave Beach.

Chapter Twelve

Back at the lagoon, Alfie stayed awake for hours. He sat on a low branch with legs dangling, keeping close watch over Pearl in the water below.

The sun sank and the sky changed from red to grey. All colour faded from the quiet scene as a large, pale moon rose above the mangrove swamp. A million bright stars shone.

Pearl stayed peacefully in the shallow water, eyes open, flippers sculling gently to stay afloat. Even in the dark, Alfie could make out the deep gash in her side – though it looked nasty, it didn't appear to cause too much pain.

The moon rose higher and seemed to grow smaller. Alfie had read that this wasn't actually true – the moon stayed the same size all through the night but it was something to do with the angle between you and it as the earth slowly tilted on its axis. He had a long time to stare at it and work it out, noticing the shadowy craters in its silver surface and wondering what it must have been like more than fifty years ago for the first person to set foot on its bare, dusty surface. He got so carried away thinking about it that he didn't pay attention to the changing tide.

The first thing he noticed was the sound of water washing more strongly against the tree roots surrounding him and Pearl. Then he saw that the water level in the lagoon had risen by as much as a metre and that large fish rose to the surface to feed on gliding insects. There would be a quiet *pop* as the fish opened its mouth to swallow then a *plop* followed by widening ripples as it disappeared. Beside him, Pearl rocked gently in the moonlight as the waves lapped against the nearby bank.

'Hey, are you hungry?' Alfie suddenly realized that the injured Pearl probably hadn't eaten for ages. 'I can do something about that,' he decided at once. So he took his knife from his waistband and studied the overhanging branches until he spotted one that was straight and strong. He reached up and cut it free. Stripping it of its leaves, he then grabbed hold of a low-hanging creeper and cut out a section that he could use to bind the knife to the end of the stick. After this, he attached another, longer length of creeper to the blunt end so that he could launch the spear then haul the prey back in. 'Look – a harpoon!' He grinned as he showed Pearl his new weapon. 'I can use it to catch fish for you.'

She clicked out a reply and sidled up to him for a stroke before he launched out into the middle of the lagoon.

He swam slowly across the smooth, silvered surface, into a cloud of tiny insects that caught in his hair and brushed against his cheeks. All the time he tried to work out how he might catch a fish big enough to satisfy Pearl's hunger – a tarpon perhaps. It was no good out here in the middle of the pond, he soon realized. He had to be able to corner the fish somehow – maybe trap it against the barrier that he and Fleur had built. Holding the harpoon clear of the water, he swam on.

Sure enough, he found fish exactly where he wanted them to be – close to the roughly constructed stockade. In the first rays of dawn light he could make out a small shoal of bright angelfish close to the surface and a shadowy, mottled grey tarpon beneath them. Alfie approached slowly and raised the harpoon above his head then took aim and threw. It disturbed the angelfish but fell short of the tarpon. He pulled it back and tried again – twice, three times until the slow-moving quarry realized the danger and disappeared among the tree roots. Meanwhile, the water level rose and the push of the incoming tide against the barrier grew stronger.

Alfie had failed in his first attempts to find food for Pearl but he didn't give up. Instead, he perched on a tree root close to the entrance to the lagoon, throwing the harpoon and improving his aim every time a fish swam through the gaps in the barrier. At last he speared a snapper and swam back triumphantly to Pearl. 'Look what I've got for you,' he told her.

She opened her mouth eagerly and swallowed the snapper then slowly ventured out from the bank. She

161

stopped in the middle of the pond and blew out noisily through her blowhole, as if to say, *Look at me – I'm feeling stronger already!*

Alfie nodded and clapped his hands. 'Cool, but take it easy,' he warned, slapping the surface to keep her attention. 'Come back here and wait for me to find you more food.'

Pearl did as she was told. She seemed happy for him to fish for her and stayed by the bank while Alfie swam back to the barrier. This time he brought back a nice big tarpon which she caught between her jaws then swallowed whole.

Flushed with success, he returned once more to the barrier. Sure, he was a bit worried by the way the tide pushed hard against it and loosened some of the rocks at its base. He and Fleur might have to do some repair work when she came back. But for now he would concentrate on finding food for Pearl.

Treading water, he turned his back and peered down below the surface. Behind him, a fresh surge of seawater forced its way over the top of the barrier into the lagoon. Then, without warning and with a sudden, sickening splintering of the wooden planks, a section of the stockade came crashing down and the shark appeared. It bulldozed through the wall with its blunt head, its dark blue back gleaming in the dawn light, its small eyes fixed on Alfie.

He spun round in time to see it open its jaws. Without thinking, he launched the harpoon and watched the flash of the blade as it soared through the air. The blade landed with a sickening thud in front of the shark's dorsal fin. The creature flicked its tail flukes and twisted in the water, giving Alfie enough time to catch hold of a branch and haul himself out of the water.

With the blade still sticking out of its back, the shark turned on him and attacked again. Desperately Alfie reached for a loose rock resting on some tree roots and heaved it high in the air before sending it crashing down on the shark's head. Again he hit his target but the stunned shark came at him a third time. Alfie hurled another rock then threw himself sideways as the advancing shark sank its teeth into the branch where he'd been perching. With a loud cry Alfie overbalanced and fell backwards into a tangle of roots, leaving the wounded shark disoriented and thrashing its tail.

There was no way that the shark's jaws could reach him now, Alfie realized. But, wounded or not, the coast was clear for it to swim across the lagoon and attack Pearl. He couldn't let that happen so he clambered over the roots towards it, determined to pound it with more rocks before it had a chance to recover.

The shark writhed in the water until the entire barrier collapsed and the full force of the tide was unleashed. A strong wave thrust the shark against a boulder, trapping it under a ledge. It writhed again and made the foaming water churn.

Then, out of nowhere, Fleur appeared on top of the boulder. She took in the scene at a glance – saw the injured shark as it struggled to swim clear of the overhang and Alfie raising a large rock and aiming it at the shark's head. She too picked up a heavy rock. She stood directly above the shark and flung it down with all the force she possessed.

Fleur's rock struck it between the eyes. It stopped struggling as a wave broke over its head. Fleur and

Alfie held their breaths. They saw the tidal rush of water retreat down the channel and in amongst the foam and shattered planks they picked out the stunned and wounded shark. They watched in silence as it was carried away from the lagoon, out to sea.

*

'The full moon was bright,' Fleur explained. 'I couldn't bear to wait any longer so I decided to set off before dawn.'

She'd lain awake all night in George's Cave, nerves stretched to their limit. George had perched close to the entrance and watched her toss and turn. Mia and James had slept fitfully while Katie had manned Lookout Point.

'It's a good job you got here early.' Sitting with Fleur on top of the boulder at the entrance to the lagoon, Alfie took a while to get over the shock of doing battle with the enemy. He would never forget the moment when the barrier had crashed down and he'd come face to face with the tiger shark.

She nodded and smiled.

'I dread to think what would've happened …' He tailed

off then slid down into the water. 'Anyway, you did.'

Fleur joined him in the water and they started to swim across the lagoon. 'Do you think it's going to be OK – the shark, I mean?'

'Dunno. Maybe it was just stunned.'

'I hope so.' In spite of everything, she couldn't bear the idea that the magnificent creature might be dead and that they were the ones who killed it.

'I did notice it moving its tail as the water carried it away.'

'Did you? Oh, good.'

Alfie couldn't help laughing. 'Honestly, what are you like?'

'Why – what do you mean?'

'That thing just tried to kill us and now you're feeling sorry for it!'

'I am,' she agreed. 'It was only doing what comes naturally – hunting prey that it can eat to stay alive.' Laughing with him, partly out of relief that they had emerged unscathed, she clung on to the hope that the shark would survive. Then, as they reached the far bank, she quickly changed the subject. 'I brought water and fruit for you. I left them in a safe place. We can go back for them later.'

'Cool.'

'I'll say hi to Pearl first.' She smiled as Alfie's friendly dolphin emerged from her leafy refuge and swam to greet them. 'Hey, Pearl – how are you doing?'

Pearl gave a low whistle and smacked her tail on the surface.

'You're doing great, aren't you?'

She clicked then rocked sideways and flapped her flipper in the air.

'Yes, I can see you are.'

'I fed her a snapper and a tarpon,' Alfie chipped in. 'That's what the harpoon was for.'

They petted Pearl for a while and promised her more fish.

'But first we have to build that barrier again,' Alfie said. 'Just in case.'

'And I have to give you your breakfast,' Fleur remembered.

It was hard to tear themselves away from Pearl but after more pats and strokes they left her wallowing in the shallow water and got to work. This time they chose sturdier branches for the stockade and rammed them even deeper into the sand. They piled heavy rocks at their base then criss-crossed the uprights with strong branches and roots.

'We have to finish this before the tide turns.' Alfie paused to check on Pearl then ducked his face in the water to cool down.

'You need to drink,' Fleur decided before hurrying away.

She waded under the branches towards the bright light of the open beach, intent on fetching water for Alfie and fruit for him to eat. As she emerged from the mangroves, she straightened up and eased her aching back. Now where exactly had she left the bag of supplies? Ah, yes – it was on a flat rock halfway down the beach ... Fleur stopped and stared.

Two capuchin monkeys stared back at her. One held a plastic water bottle to its mouth while the other had ripped open the bag and started to gobble jackfruit.

'No – stop that!' Fleur waved her arms at the furry thieves.

The first one tipped the bottle and poured water over its face. The other crammed more fruit into its mouth.

'I said, stop!' She sprinted towards them. 'Those are for Alfie. Stop right now!'

Chapter Thirteen

Fleur shooed the monkeys away and rescued what was left of the fruit and water. She carried them back to Alfie who had already set about catching a breakfast snapper for Pearl. By the time the sun was up they were hard at work building a new barrier and an hour or two later they had some surprise visitors.

'Hiya, you two!' Mia was the first to jump down from the ledge under Magic Arch on to the beach in Mangrove Bay. She was quickly followed by James and Katie.

Fleur and Alfie were taking a break, sunning themselves on the rock where the capuchin monkeys had snuck up and captured their supplies. They waved then ran to meet Mia and their mum and dad.

'Why are you here?' Alfie demanded.

'We're making sure that you're both OK.' Mia flung herself at him and hugged him. 'Fleur left George's Cave before we woke up. She didn't say goodbye.'

'Everything's cool. We're fine.'

'I knew you would be,' Mia confided as she stepped away and held up the mother-of-pearl dolphin that hung around her neck. ''Cos I was wearing my lucky charm.'

A smiling Fleur realized how fortunate she and Alfie had been to survive the shark attack. 'And, guess what – it really works!'

'Have you seen the shark lately?' James got down to serious business as he strode up the beach.

Reluctant to admit the truth, Fleur closed her eyes and wrinkled her nose. 'Actually ...'

'Yes!' Alfie confessed.

When Katie joined them she took food, water and new straw hats out of a plastic bag then made everyone sit in a circle. She jammed Alfie's hat on his head and gave him a serious look. 'OK, what's the story?'

So they told her about the shark attack without leaving out any details.

When it came to the part about the shark crashing

171

through the stockade, Mia's mouth fell open and she gasped. 'What happened to Pearl? Is she OK?'

Alfie nodded. He stood up and told them to come and see for themselves.

So they all waded up the channel and under the tunnel of mangrove trees until they came to the entrance to the lagoon.

'This is our new barrier,' Alfie said proudly. 'It's not finished yet but it's going to be better than the first one.'

His dad tested one of the uprights for sturdiness. 'Good job,' he murmured. 'And you've left gaps for the seawater to flow in and out – that's a good idea.'

'And here's our hospital pool for Pearl until she gets better.' Fleur swam ahead of them towards the far bank, glad to see that Alfie's dolphin was coming to meet them.

'Hey, Pearl!' Mia lifted her hand clear of the water and waved.

Pearl disappeared below the surface then came up to say hello. She rocked sideways to let them see the shark bite then blew a loud raspberry through her blowhole.

'That's what she thinks of the tiger shark.' Alfie's remark made everyone burst out laughing, then Katie swam up alongside Fleur, the dolphin expert.

'How long will that wound take to heal?' she asked.

'It should be pretty quick – maybe another day or two.'

'And, Alfie, I take it that you want to stick around until Pearl's better?' Katie swam towards a mangrove root and hauled herself out of the water. 'Silly question; I don't know why I bothered to ask. That means the rest of us will have to keep you supplied with food and water every few hours but that shouldn't be a problem. And I guess we'll have to do without you at base camp for a little while.'

James joined Katie on the root. With his long legs dangling in the water, he drew himself upright and gave a salute. 'Lance Corporal Alfie Fisher, you're officially relieved of shelter building duties.'

'Yessir!' Alfie saluted back then backflipped and did an underwater somersault.

'And all your other duties,' Katie agreed when he came up for air. 'But only until Pearl is better. Then it'll be back to collecting firewood, putting the roof on the shelter and finishing that canoe.'

✽

The days and nights of Alfie's vigil were long and calm. The sun rose and set in clear skies. The cool moon cast its silver light on the still surface of the lagoon. On the third day Pearl began to catch her own fish and on the next day she started to push with her beak against the wooden barricade.

'I think she's ready to leave,' Fleur observed when she and Mia brought fresh food supplies. It was late in the afternoon. The low sun cast long shadows across the shimmering water.

They sat together on the mangrove roots close to the entrance, enjoying the sight of Pearl rolling and smacking her tail against the surface. Then she came up to Alfie and rested her head on his knees.

He stroked her softly. 'Are you?' he murmured with a hint of sadness in his voice.

Pearl gave a low whistle then nudged his leg. *I'm ready*.

'Don't be sad, Alfie.' Mia slid into the water. 'Pearl

isn't sick any more. That should make you happy.'

Fleur saw that the damaged flesh on Pearl's flank had almost knitted back together. 'That's amazing,' she breathed as she lowered herself into the water to pat her. Then, following one of her mysterious 'feelings', she stepped from one root to another until she emerged from the mangroves on to a high boulder overlooking Mangrove Bay. She climbed up for a better view of the beach and the sea beyond.

'Oh, wow!' To make sure that her hunch had been right, she shaded her eyes and looked again. Yes, it was true – a dolphin pod was swimming under Magic Arch and into the bay. They arrived two or three at a time, riding the waves with ease then seeking out calmer water in the middle of the bay. And who surged under the arch last of all then leaped clear in perfect unison? It was none other than Jazz and Stormy.

Fleur cried out with joy. 'Alfie, Mia, guess who's here.' She clapped her hands and shouted. 'Hiya, Stormy, hiya, Jazz – am I glad to see you!'

The two youngsters swam quickly towards the shore. They clicked and whistled excitedly.

'And I know who else will be,' Fleur told them as she scrambled from the boulder and back through the mangroves to find the others. 'Dolphins!' she gasped at Alfie and Mia.

'Where?' Mia demanded.

'Out there in the bay. Jazz and Stormy and the whole pod. They're waiting for Pearl. Quick, Alfie – we have to knock the barrier down.'

He took a deep breath then reached out to give Pearl one last stroke. 'Can you hear them calling you?' he whispered.

She rolled in the water then gave a loud whistle. There was a faint reply: a shrill call from Stormy and a high-low signal from Jazz.

Alfie nodded. 'OK, let's do this,' he said to Mia and Fleur.

Together they wrenched at the planks and branches that formed the stockade. Alfie swam underwater to dislodge the rocks. Fleur and Mia pulled and pushed until the barrier finally came down.

Then Pearl swam eagerly through the narrow gap into the channel that led to the sea. She made her birdlike whistle and turned her head towards Alfie, Fleur and Mia. *Come with me.*

They followed her, rushed along by the tidal pull of the water until they reached the sea.

Ahead of them, the first waves broke over Pearl's back. Then the water lifted her and carried her out towards Jazz and Stormy who greeted her by swimming close and rubbing their beaks against her. In the background, the rest of the pod celebrated the reunion by leaping high in the air.

Alfie steadied himself as waves crashed around him. He managed to stand up and wait for Fleur and Mia who tumbled through the water after him. Together they held hands and watched Pearl's pod surround her. Marina came alongside her calf then swam with her around the circle of dolphins, all clicking and whistling their own greetings. But it was Jazz and Stormy who made the most noise, twisting and turning and blowing bubbles before rising in spectacular tail-walks under Magic Arch.

Pearl left her mother's side and followed them. She raised herself out of the water and copied them, flapping her flippers as she went.

'Yep – she's better,' Fleur said with a long, contented sigh.

Mia laughed and tapped her charm. 'Lucky, lucky, lucky!'

With tears in his eyes, Alfie watched Pearl swim with her pod around the southern headland. He was proud that he'd looked after her so well. It meant they were equal somehow. But he would miss her more than he could say. 'Bye, Pearl,' he murmured. 'See you soon.'

There was no reply.

Far out to sea, as the sun set, the dolphins rode the swell of waves that broke against the shores of Misty Island. They breached the water and soared in high, perfect arcs then plunged deep amongst shoals of silversides. They wove between coral reefs and through forests of sea grass, across countless miles of clear, sparkling ocean.

The story
continues
in ...

Turn the
page for a
sneak peek ...

Chapter One

Boo!' Mia Fisher crept up on her older brother, Alfie, while he was sleeping under a palm tree.

He awoke with a sudden jerk then sprang to his feet. 'That's not funny!' he yelled after her as she sprinted down the beach.

'Can't catch me!' she cried over her shoulder.

'Seriously, Mia – don't.' Alfie was unhappy as he brushed sand from his red shorts and jammed his straw hat more firmly on his head. 'You're always doing stuff like that; making me jump and scaring me to death.'

His thirteen-year-old sister, Fleur, slowly opened one eye and then the other. 'She's seven. Annoying people is what seven-year-olds do.' Once she was sure that Mia had stopped at the water's edge, she closed her eyes and carried on with her siesta.

'She'd better not do it again.' Eleven-year-old Alfie went on grumbling as he left the shade of the palm tree and walked towards the family shelter built out of bamboo canes and palm leaves. The sturdy structure was raised on stilts and had a platform made from salvaged wooden planks thrown up on to the beaches of Dolphin Island at high tide. The thatched roof was secured with old rope and lianas from the tropical jungle that covered the high mountain peak at the centre of the island. The Fishers had built their home strongly to stand up to hurricane force winds that swept in off the blue ocean, often hitting without warning and tearing up most things that lay in their path. Alfie climbed on to the platform and watched through narrowed eyes as Mia cavorted along the shoreline.

She laughed as a wave broke against nearby rocks and she felt the cool spray shower down over her head. She danced through the foam that swirled around her ankles then she cartwheeled back up the beach towards him. 'Play I-spy!' she clamoured. 'I spy with my little eye something beginning with ...'

'No way,' Alfie mumbled, disappearing inside the shelter as she drew near.

'It's OK, Mia – I'll play.' Fleur sat up with a sigh. She wiggled her toes in the warm white sand and glanced out to sea to check for dolphins. The calm blue water sparkled on without interruption, out past the reef where their yacht, *Merlin*, had sunk and onwards to the dazzling, flat horizon.

'Yay! ... Something beginning with M!'

'Mountain?'

'Nope.'

'Millipede?' Fleur pointed to a reddish-brown specimen with black spots undulating up a nearby tree trunk. She calculated that it was at least twenty centimetres long.

'No.'

'Mum?'

'No. Anyway, you can't see her. She's at Lookout Point with Dad.'

Fair enough. 'OK, I give in.'

'Monkey!' Mia lifted her hat to reveal her furry friend. She tossed him high in the air and attempted to catch him but he landed in the sand at Fleur's feet.

'Poor Monkey.' Fleur picked him up and dusted him down. The battered soft toy, a survivor of shipwreck, storm and fire, had only one eye and a bald patch on top of his head. Fleur held him to her chest and pretended to cuddle him.

Suddenly serious, Mia knelt down beside her. After more than seven weeks on the island, her brown hair had turned blonde at the tips and her hazel eyes shone brightly in her round, tanned face. Around her neck she wore a mother-of-pearl charm in the shape of a dolphin and she had a string of shells around her waist over a turquoise swimsuit that had faded to pale blue. 'I've got a cool idea,' she said to Fleur. 'We could make an eyepatch for Monkey.'

'I guess we could,' Fleur's answer was cautious and the corners of her mouth twitched as she tried not to smile. 'It might make him look like a pirate though.'

'Hmm.' Mia tilted her head to one side to consider this. 'Yay, a pirate!' She snatched the toy monkey from Fleur then sprinted towards the shelter. 'Alfie, guess what – we're going to make an eyepatch for Monkey.

He'll be a pirate!'

Animal-mad Fleur let the smile appear. *Cute*, she thought as she rested back on her elbows. *But give me a real live monkey any day.*

She lay back in the sand and stared up at the palm leaf canopy. Seven weeks on Dolphin Island felt like a whole lifetime. It seemed an age since *Merlin* had been caught in a storm in the Torres Strait and had capsized in the mountainous waves. Fleur relived the fear that she'd felt when she, Alfie and Mia had scrambled up on deck just in time, only to be tossed overboard without knowing what had happened to Katie and James, their mum and dad, or whether the current would sweep them to dry land or further out to sea. And then the magical moment when their dolphins had appeared out of nowhere; three grey, domed heads emerging from the waves, whistling and clicking above the roaring wind, as if each one was saying, *Grab my fin. Hold on tight!* She remembered the miracle that was Pearl, Jazz and Stormy carrying them all safely to the shore.

Fleur took a deep breath then let out a loud sigh.

The Fisher family had come through so much since then. They'd landed on the uninhabited island and found shelter in George's Cave. The storm had passed and the next day Mum and Dad had found them and there'd been a happy reunion. They'd all pulled together to build a rough shelter and find fresh water at Butterfly Falls. They'd lit a fire and learned how to fish with the help of their faithful dolphin friends when Jazz, Stormy and Pearl had swum into the bay and driven shoals of silver fish into Fleur and Alfie's primitive net.

And that had only been the beginning. Ships, boats and planes had passed without noticing the smoke from their fires or their pleas for help written in giant letters in the wet sand. Hopes of rescue had risen then faded like the trail of vapour left behind by the planes. There'd been more storms, plus a fire started by marauding macaque monkeys that had destroyed their first shelter and all their belongings, then finally a shark attack that had left Alfie's precious Pearl fighting for survival. *So much!* Fleur thought with a sigh.

The life that she'd lived before Dolphin Island now

seemed unreal. Once upon a time she'd gone to school and hung out with friends. She'd washed her hair whenever she'd wanted, followed fashions and watched YouTube videos. She'd seen capuchin monkeys and tree kangaroos on wildlife documentaries but never until now in real life.

It was the same for Alfie. He'd been a maths geek and techie, and he'd known everything about the navigation system aboard *Merlin*. Now he used a stick of charcoal to draw a map of Dolphin Island on sailcloth and carved notches on to a calendar stick to mark off the days.

Thursday. Day 53. It felt like for ever.

'Fleur, look at this!' Mia jumped down from the platform and ran towards her, holding Monkey aloft. 'Alfie did it. He made him an eyepatch out of a blue plastic bottle top and a piece of string he found on Turtle Beach. It's so cool! Look!'